PRAISE FOR *FINL*

T0267415

"Doktorski (How My Summer W
humorous banter with teenage hijinks and heartfelt conversations to deliver a propulsive road-trip novel that showcases white-cued characters refusing to be defined by their hardships forging new paths forward."

—*Publishers Weekly* starred review

"A sardonic, funny, heart-warming postcard from the ever-elusive land of normal. Perfectionist Gemma and sporty Lucas invite us on a wild road-trip escape, filled with camping, milky coffee, greasy diners, heart-to-hearts, an adopted raccoon, and grungy motel rooms, as they learn together that the heart is a muscle that needs to be fed."

—Colby Cedar Smith, author of the verse novels *The Siren and the Star* and *Call Me Athena*

"A riveting tale of two not-so-'normal' teens (and a baby raccoon) who are on the lam and heading across the country toward self-discovery, self-acceptance and each other. Funny, edgy and touching, *Finding Normal* is a can't-miss read."

—Val Emmich, *New York Times* bestselling author of *Dear Evan Hansen: The Novel*

"If only getting where you wanted to be in life could be as easy as pointing to a spot on the map and following an already-laid-out course. But Lucas and Gemma teach us that such a journey is important, to a great extent, because each one of us has to chart the path ourselves. Doktorski's voice is equal parts funny and real, and as a reader, you'll be more than glad to be along on her characters' life-changing ride."

—Holly Schindler, award-winning author of *A Blue So Dark*

"On a road trip to *Finding Normal*, Gemma and Lucas build a deep friendship that leads them someplace neither of them ever could have imagined."

—J. Albert Mann, award-winning author of *The Degenerates*

FINDING NORMAL

Jennifer Salvato Doktorski

Fitzroy Books

Published by Fitzroy Books
An imprint of
Regal House Publishing, LLC
Raleigh, NC 27605
All rights reserved

https://fitzroybooks.com
Printed in the United States of America

ISBN -13 (paperback): 9781646035632
ISBN -13 (epub): 9781646035649
Library of Congress Control Number: 2024935070

Cover images and design by © C. B. Royal

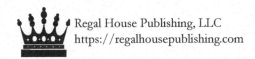

Regal House Publishing, LLC
https://regalhousepublishing.com

Printed in the United States of America

For every Gemma and Lucas.
You deserve to be seen.
You deserve to be understood.
You deserve to be loved.

1

Skinny is a place. At least I thought it was.

One I fought through dizzy spells, hair loss, and freezing extremities to get to, because getting to Skinny would make everything better, right? Wrong. I never got there.

Instead, I landed myself here. Here, being the eating disorder floor at Children's Hospital in Harrisburg, Pennsylvania. Or as the staff refers to it, River House. Like it's summer camp and we're here by choice, not being held against our will.

It's Sunday night and the common room is empty except for the perpetually distracted med student assigned to babysit me. He taps his keyboard with an annoying, erratic rhythm that makes me want to smash his laptop against the wall. The only other sound is the hum of the refrigerator packed with the high-calorie juices and Boost shakes used to fatten us up.

"Ten more minutes, Genna," he says.

"Gemma." I correct him for the millionth fucking time.

I used to think doctors were ridiculously smart. Turns out, they're just like the rest of us. Tacking that onto my list of life's great disappointments.

"Sorry, Gemma," he says, emphasizing the MMs this time. Dick.

"Uh-huh." I don't bother looking up from my *Rand McNally Road Atlas*. I've been scouring its pages for the last forty minutes, from Abbeville, Alabama, to Wright, Wyoming, searching for Skinny. They confiscated my phone when I got here so there isn't much else to do. They think technology is trying to kill us. I think the disconnection will.

While looking for Skinny I discovered two towns named Joy. One called Dismal, four named Lucky, two Borings, and seventeen Freedoms. Then I discovered something even more interesting.

There are *five* towns in the United States named Normal.

After three weeks in the hospital, where my every move from shitting to staring at a goddamn map is watched, I now have this incredible urge to run there. Normal. A base camp to catch my breath before scaling the summit to Skinny.

I write down the approximate distances between Harrisburg and each Normal in my notebook, leaving extra lines in between to add information.

Normal, Alabama, 750 miles.

Normal, Illinois, 730 miles.

Normal, Indiana, 580 miles.

Normal, Kentucky, 420 miles.

Normal, Tennessee, 900 miles.

I can visit them all. I *will* visit them all. If for no other reason than to prove everyone wrong. Of all the words used to describe me, "normal" has never been one of them.

I'll send postcards. "Greetings from Normal, bitches. I made it!" Okay, maybe not. I've never once had the occasion to say "bitches" out loud. But first, I have to get out of here.

"If they can't get our names right, makes you wonder what else they don't know," says a voice beside my table. "Am I right?"

A guy, the first I've seen with an inpatient bracelet like mine, stands there waiting for me to acknowledge him.

He points his chin toward my atlas. "Planning an escape?"

"*No*," I say, like it's the most absurd thing I've ever heard.

I spread my fingers protectively over Illinois. Other than mandatory group sessions, which I lie my way through, I've pretty much been the president and sole member of the Anti-Social Club after passing out in gym class and winding up here.

"Don't worry, I won't tell. If you take me with you."

I scan his muscular but slight V-shaped frame, and weigh him with my eyes. Is he mocking me? He smiles, revealing a chipped front tooth. Cute. But I'm not falling for it.

"Wrestler?" Lightweight, no doubt.

His eyes widen, raising the veil on his overconfidence. He

seems young. Younger than me, at least. But I'm a seven-teen-year-old in a prepubescent body, so who knows?

"How'd you—?"

"I can spot a slave to the scale when I see one. Plus, you're here, aren't you?"

I make a panoramic sweep with my arm. Vanna revealing the prize puzzle.

Chipped Tooth doesn't say anything. A moment later, it's clear he was assessing me too. "Straight As, AP everything, 1500 on the SAT?"

"1530." I can't stop myself.

"I know Extra when I see it."

I bristle. Extra. That's what kids at school call me. Not in a good way. In way that's supposed to make me ashamed that my endless pursuit of perfection knows no bounds. I was born without an "off" switch. Presentation posters become my *Mona Lisa*. Term papers, my magnum opus. My therapist at the hospital, Dr. Paige Bryant, likes to call it "sticky brain." Why can't she just say it's OCD on overdrive or something? Whatever.

I hate her. Hate everything about her. From her conde-scending tone to the way she flips her long black hair like she's in a goddamn shampoo commercial. Like she knows it's exactly what mine looked like before it fell out in lusterless clumps and I lopped the rest off with craft scissors. Oh, and then there's her insistence that I call her Dr. Bryant, not Paige as I've been known to do. Like she's some kind of real doctor. She thinks she knows all about "girls like me," spouting her fortune cookie advice like I shit my brain out with laxatives.

Bad things happen when you don't eat.

The scale tells the tale.

It's not your size, it's about all the wonderful things a healthy body can do.

Fuck. You.

Must be nice getting paid to point out the obvious. "Cliches and Platitudes" must be a core requirement for psych majors.

The chair makes a rib-rattling sound as Chipped Tooth pulls it out and plops down.

"Mind if I sit?"

"You already did, and yes, I do."

He circles his hands like he's polishing the air in front of him.

"I'm detecting a definite loner vibe here. Maybe a touch of hostility."

Did my "Love Dogs Hate People" T-shirt not give it away?

I mimic him, hand gestures and all. "I'm detecting a there-must-be-some-mistake-I-don't-belong-here vibe."

That wipes the sunshine off his face. "I *don't* belong here."

An ironic laugh escapes my lips. I almost feel bad for him. Almost. "Know what? Me either."

Here's the thing. I really don't. I'm not like the others here. I don't have a *disease*, I'm just really, really good at dieting. Better than those girls in my AP bio lab who talk a good game with their Keto bars and baby carrots. They gave up after a few weeks. I couldn't turn the switch off.

"Gemma." Dr. Dumbass nudges me with his tone from the far side of the room.

I slam my atlas closed and stand up. Chipped Tooth's attempt to cajole me into conversation has failed. More than jaded, I'm a charred lump of coal.

He's the kind of guy who never talked to me when I was fat. He's the kind of guy I won't talk to now.

"Table's all yours," I say, hoping he feels the breeze as I rush by him on my way out the door.

2

Solitaire is a lonely game.

Unlike chess or gin rummy, where opponents face off in battle.

Solitaire is one person's private war against the cards they're dealt.

Most days my roommate, Monika, reaches for her fifty-two-card deck the moment she wakes up and adds her incessant card shuffling to the chorus of ambient hospital sounds I endure every day. The heart monitor, the din of voices at the nurses' station, the elevator's ping outside our door. Only her cards are much, much louder and infinitely more irritating.

It's only lunchtime and she's been at it for hours.

She's not fooling me. It's not about winning. It's about burning calories. I sense her back there behind the curtain she keeps drawn between us like the Great Wall of China, jiggling her legs, clenching her abs, glutes, and any other muscles she has left to contract, as she peels back the edges of the deck and prepares to let the cards rip.

"Can you please shuffle quietly?"

Monika shuffles louder.

I'd call her on it if her silence didn't scare the crap out of me. This is my first time away from home and I've never shared a room with anyone before. So, even though it's totally not my comfort zone, I've tried several times to have a real conversation. Especially back when I first got here and I was scared, and lonely, and had this naive idea she needed someone as much as I did, maybe more. We inhabit the same space, breathe the same air. We fight the same fight in different ways though it's hard to say which one of us is winning.

But even basic small talk, like "What are you watching?" elicits a vacant stare from her preternaturally large sunken eyes, forcing my gaze to shift to the tube protruding from her left nostril, used by the nurses to send food down her throat. It's the only time I hear Monika's voice. Her whimpering and quiet repetition of "no, please, no" rip through me like a hollow-tip bullet. Her pain comes not from the process, but from the knowledge she's been fed.

It's heartbreaking.

And yet weirdly comforting, knowing I'm not as afraid of eating as her, and because of that, I still have some control.

Monika got here before me, before anyone else on the floor it seems, and commandeered the room's window side and the sunlight that comes along with it. The shades stay closed all day, every day, leaving me to wither under dim fluorescent lighting or else prop open the door and lose all vestiges of privacy.

I roll my tray table away from the bed, adjust it to meet my chair's height, and turn back to the page in my well-worn atlas where I left off before Chipped Tooth interrupted my precious solitude last night.

Ever since I was little, I've needed to know where I am and where I'm going, like there's a geolocator in my brain that needs constant resetting. My dad, a reluctant flier since his army days, planned themed road trips for me and Mom every summer. National Parks one year, amusement parks the next. Mom was our navigator.

This atlas was hers. She'd owned it since her spring break trip to Florida, back when she was in college. Before GPS and cars with touchscreens. As soon as I could read, she'd let me page through it in the car. I loved its heft. The way it fell across my lap, covering my thighs and knees, like a weighted blanket. I'd stretch out in the backseat highlighting all the roads we traveled; those faded yellow lines lead to memories now, of Dad playing drums on the steering wheel, Mom reading *People* magazine with her bare feet propped up on the dash.

Dad bequeathed it to me after Mom died and it has been my talisman ever since. I found it sandwiched between layers of clothes in the suitcase he brought me from home. I'm not sure why. Dad and I haven't been anywhere together in forever. I do the math in my head. Breaking out of here will be my first road adventure in six years.

I locate the circled star over Harrisburg and use my pointer finger to trace the westward leading roads and highways. New territory for me. No highlights. Using the map's scale, I calculate the distance to the Ohio state line, the way Mom taught me. At home, I'm all about Google Maps, but like I said here in River House technology, with the exception of game shows, a few approved sitcoms, and HGTV on the wall-mounted flatscreen, is "strictly prohibited."

They want us to avoid the triggers lurking on social media like images of skeletal social media influencers that show up in our news feeds and the plated meals we abhor on The Food Network. Are they going to child-proof the whole world for me when I'm finally discharged? Triggers are everywhere. In books. High school cafeterias. Fro-yo places in LA, apparently.

But what really makes me want to pull what's left of my hair out is that I desperately need my laptop to finish and send my college apps.

The nurses' aide pushes the door open with her butt and backs into the room with my lunch tray.

"Make some room, honey."

Maeve nods toward my map but may as well be talking about my stomach. I'm still full from my mid-morning "snack." A bagel and cream cheese, fruit cup, and apple juice, which no one above the age of three actually drinks. So much food. Our rooms constantly smell like disinfectant and the school cafeteria.

She sets the tray down, then pulls up a chair to face me. She gets paid to watch me eat. Good times.

"Got those potato stars today that you like so much!"

I like nothing here. Food is the enemy. Fat and carbs sent in like star-shaped Trojan horses. But I thank Maeve anyway. She's one of the nicest aides on the floor and was assigned to me because I'm a compliant eater.

"A clean plate ranger," my grandmother used to call me when I was little. When we visited, she'd make all my favorites, chicken cutlets, mashed potatoes, lemon meringue pie. I inhaled it all like oxygen. It's no wonder I was a chubby kid.

The thought of a heavy meal like that disgusts me now. At some point I discovered an empty stomach made my life fuller. I had more time to be Extra, and less to feel lonely. With every lost pound, I became stronger, unstoppable. Until I blacked out when my head thudded against the gym floor and woke up here, where no one cares that I'd rather be hungry than fat.

Maeve turns on the wall-mounted TV with the remote. "Let's catch the end of *The Price is Right*," she says. Maeve loves game shows and soap operas. I can't even.

I dip a potato star in ketchup and take a bite. Unlike Monika, I'm not sick. Within a day after being admitted, I figured out the fastest way out and back to dieting was to eat whatever they put in front of me. That includes today's lunch of tater-tot-like stars and six chicken tenders, a salad with creamy Italian dressing, two cups of ice cream, and an extra-tall glass of whole milk. I tally the calories in my head.

Gross. How could all these so-called medical profession-als not know that humans, like all other mammals, should be weaned from dairy products by the time they get their teeth?

Two hours from now they'll bring me an afternoon snack, then dinner, then a snack before lights out. I stopped counting the calories in my head. It's too depressing. If we don't eat ev-erything, we're given the caloric equivalent in chalky nutritional drinks. If we don't drink up, we get tubed, like Monika. Their methods are draconian, not to mention dehumanizing.

But I smile at Maeve and swallow my chicken tenders. They taste like greasy, batter-dipped pounds sliding down my throat, gagging me. But I chase it with milk and bide my time.

"Bid $501!" Maeve coaches the on-screen contestant.

Let them try to fatten me up like the witch did with Hansel and Gretel. If those crafty lederhosen-clad kids played along and escaped, then so can I.

3

After every meal, much like preschoolers and the elderly, we nap. Or try to. Even if we don't sleep, we must lay in bed for thirty minutes.

"Gotta repair those muscles and organs," Maeve said to me my first week here.

"I've never had muscles," I said.

"The heart is a muscle," she said.

"What's your point?" I asked.

That day, Maeve shot me a look that told me to zip it. So I closed my eyes, imagined my metabolic rate slowing to that of a sloth, and accepted my fate as a post-meal napper.

I've become an expert at feigning sleep to escape conversation with my nurse's aide, who stays after meals to make sure I don't walk around or attempt to use the bathroom. They have nothing to worry about. I'm a dieter, not a purger, though this place might turn me into one.

"There's a music class today in the common room," Maeve blurts out. She knows I'm playing possum and that she's the only aide I like talking to.

"I hate music." I open my eyes but keep my back to her.

"Come on now, stop talking nonsense. No one hates music. It's unnatural."

So is having someone stare at me while I eat. But ya know. Here we are.

"How about art?"

I moan. Maeve never indulges my complaints. Being upbeat seems to be her life's mission. I cannot relate.

"Yoga?" Maeve tries.

"That stupid stretching class? That's not yoga. It's lying down on the floor and breathing. No one breaks a sweat."

At that moment, Monika rouses and immediately begins

shuffling. I'd like to liquify those cards in a blender and send them through her feeding tube. I close my eyes.

"What time is yoga?"

"One thirty." Maeve's voice is filled with smugness.

"Fine."

My stomach struggles to contain what feels like a floundering fish shimmying upstream in my esophagus. I don't have time to get hungry here. They cram food into me like those fake snakes in a can. Like a practical joke. Do they really believe making me fat will cure me? Being fat made me unhappy. Being unhappy made me diet. Dieting made me sick.

I overdid it. I get it. But who exactly are these quacks sitting around a conference table, looking over my charts and saying, "Food is her medicine. Give her carbs, give her fats, make her eat cake. Yes, that will work."

I wrap my thumb and pinky around my wrist, like a cobra eating its own tail. The tips still touch, but my fingers don't overlap anymore. I contract my stomach muscles and hold my breath, resisting the urge to lie down on the floor and do crunches, and wondering if the bruises along my spine have healed.

The door bangs open, and Maeve and I jump. Monika's mother. A petite squirrel-ish woman with dark tired eyes, she darts from one side of the room to the other, trailing the scent of cigarettes and mint gum behind her. Today, she blows by us so fast, the curtain billows upward and I catch a glimpse of Monika's stunned expression.

"Mom. What are you doing here? This isn't your day."

It's the most words I've heard from Monika since I arrived. Everything I know about Monika is from what is said *to* her, not what she says. *Do you need more MiraLax, Monika? Any scratches on your arms today? Are you still feeling that you might want to hurt yourself?* I shouldn't know that Monika is a virgin but has given blow jobs to past boyfriends, or that her dad is a recovering addict who backslid after her first hospitalization. This is her fourth.

Patient privacy laws are a joke.

Monika's mom and dad visit on alternating days, after work. I live more than two hours away and since Dad works six days a week at his garage, he mostly visits on Sundays, which is okay because it gives me something to look forward to. Weekends around here suck. Half the staff is gone and without their comings and goings to push the dense, slow-moving minutes along, time seems to fold backward, like afterschool detention in the ninth circle of hell.

By Monday morning, I'm almost begging to go to group. Or not. Group is a different kind of hell.

Monika's mom catches her breath. "I'm on my lunch break so I don't have much time. I just met with your team."

"What? Why?"

"Listen." Monika's mom lowers her voice. Maeve and I have to strain, but we can still hear. (The great HIPAA loophole.)

"You're getting out of here."

"I'm going home? Oh, Mom, thank—"

"Wait, sweetheart. Let me finish. You're not going home."

Maeve raises her eyebrows at me.

"You're leaving for a residential treatment center in Denver on Saturday. They're supposedly the best. Your father will fly out with you. Get you settled. I'll be there as soon as I can work out carpooling for your brothers and a virtual office situation for myself."

Silence, followed by card shuffling.

"Monika?"

More shuffling. Maeve and I hold our breath.

"Monika? Talk to me." Mom's tone is sharper.

"Why are you doing this to me?"

"Because I love you. Because this place isn't helping you and I'm not going to let you die. Not on my watch."

"Can't I come home first?"

"Sorry, baby."

I don't hear anything except sniffling for a long while and wonder if one or both are crying. "Okay. See you tomorrow, after work. Call me later." She exits the room with less velocity than she entered, pausing at the door before she opens it, like maybe she forgot something. It's okay. She's going to get better, I say, too soft for anyone to hear.

Then Monika's mom is gone, the door closing softly behind her.

Maeve bends toward my ear. "That's some tough Mom love."

"I guess."

I wouldn't know. My mom died when I was nine. Every year, I lose more of her to my imperfect memory. I have no idea what connotes a mother's love, tough or otherwise. But sometimes I imagine her here, every day, reading a book or watching *Friends* reruns with me like I see some parents on the floor doing.

Dad and I love each other, of course, but not in an effusive way. Mom was the hugger. Her arms encircled me like a mama goose's wings sheltering her goslings. No one has made me feel that way since. I fear no one ever will.

"Monika? I'm going to stupid yoga class today. Wanna come?"

Nothing. No sniffling. No shuffling. No screaming.

The heart is a muscle. A strong but fragile one that needs to be fed. It can withstand its share of blows, but when the fissures spread far and deep enough, eventually it will break.

4

Om.

It is the beginning and the end. A sacred sound.

"It is everything."

So says the visiting yoga instructor. Amateur. I call bullshit.

But it's better than being trapped in a room with Monika. Without me there, she won't need to bury her face in her pillow to muffle her sobs. Like she does most nights when she thinks I'm asleep. *Talk to me*, I wish I could say from my side of the ugly curtain.

"In through the nose for four, out through the nose for four," says our instructor.

Seated upright with crisscross applesauce legs and my eyes only half-closed, I press praying hands to my diaphragm and refuse to inhale through my nose. The shared yoga mats smell of disinfectant, making me wish for essential oils or, better yet, a pumpkin pie candle. Smelling foods, and food-scented things like candles and hand sanitizer, has become a thing with me. A source of pleasure I don't talk about.

Stillness is not my thing. My body fidgets and my thoughts grow agitated by my burgeoning boobs, which rest ever so slightly against my wrists. Two weeks ago, my chest was flatter than Kansas.

"Set your intention for your practice. Relax your shoulders. Feel your breath connect with your body."

Feel my boobs getting bigger. I hate them.

They arrived, along with my menstrual cycle, unannounced and unwelcomed when I was ten and wedged themselves between me and my childhood. Me and my peers. My mother's death had already forced me to grow up faster than them. *You need to buy her a bra*, I can hear the school nurse saying to my father from her office phone. *She should wear longer shirts with leggings. Her wardrobe can be distracting.* I curled into a ball to make myself smaller. Worse than what the stupid nurse said, was what kids said to me. *Gemma can be the bottom of the pyramid, there's no way she's getting on my back. You're not wearing a bikini, are you? You'd be pretty if you weren't chubby.* The memories press like sharp-edged wisdom teeth, pushing and pushing until they tear through the delicate pink flesh. I suck in my breath, tamp it all down, only vaguely aware that the class is almost over.

Our yogi transitions us to happy baby, where we lie on our backs, bend our knees, and grab our toes. The position seems more conducive to birthing happy babies than being one. My butt-bone is killing me. Enough. I drop my legs and lie flat, letting my face muscles droop toward the mat.

"Just here for the savasana, I see."

I open one eye. My gaze travels up smooth hairless legs to black shorts, a tight-fitting tank, an earnest face. Chipped Tooth. He rolls out a mat and lies next to me.

"Me too," he says.

Eyes closed again I whisper from the corner of my mouth, "I thought lying down on a mat meant defeat for wrestlers."

"I wouldn't know. I'm undefeated."

"Arrogant much?" I joke.

"I'm not bragging, it's a fact. My season starts in two weeks. I refuse to get stuck here while real life moves on without me. Know what I mean?"

It's true. We are ghosts living shadow lives. But unlike Chipped Tooth, I'm not pining for my high school life. I mean, I miss Dad and my own bed with all the faux-fur pillows, but it's not like I'd be shopping for a homecoming dress or going to parties with my friends. Being a straight-A student with four AP classes is time-consuming. I'm pining for my laptop so I don't fall farther behind.

"I should be conditioning, getting ready," he says.

I should be polishing my *Why Columbia?* essay, I think.

"I usually run three or four miles before school, hit the weight room twice a day, then practice until seven, if we don't have a match. At home it's free weights and crunches after homework and pushups before bed. I don't stop. You know?"

My god, Chipped Tooth doesn't shut up.

"I'm Lucas by the way."

Did he hear me call him Chipped Tooth in my head? I debate giving him a fake name but what would be the point. He's so damned nice, being mean would make me look like an asshole.

"Gemma."

"I know. Heard you correcting that intern, remember? These people... I'm going to lose my effing mind."

"Pff. I'm starting my fourth week. You've only been here for, like, ten seconds."

"Not true. Came in through the ER a week ago. Thought I was having a heart attack after a 10K. It was my best time too. Anyway, they transferred me here from cardiology."

"Were you?"

"Was I what?" Chipped Tooth isn't following.

"Having a heart attack?"

"Nope. Acid reflux. I'm perfectly healthy and ready to bust out of here. You in?"

At the instructor's prompt, I roll to one side and face him. This kid is in some serious denial. He wouldn't be here if he was perfectly healthy.

"You don't even know me," I say.

He's lying on his side facing me, head propped up on his hand, not even pretending to be in a yoga pose.

"I've got good instincts. It's a wrestler thing. Adept at predicting people's next moves. That's how I know you're going to run away."

I wish. "I just like looking at maps."

"Come on. I saw you studying that atlas. You weren't just killing time. You were making plans."

"Shhh!" The yogi shushes. "Please be respectful of everyone else's practice."

"What are we practicing for?" he whispers.

I smile, despite not wanting to give him the satisfaction.

"Aha. You're warming up to me, aren't you? Eventually, the Polizzi charm wins people over."

"Don't be so sure. The Polizzi charm has never met the Leonardo contrariness."

He laughs. "Oh, but I have. No worries. I like a challenge."

I turn over onto my back, hug my knees to my chest and roll to the side facing away from him. Undeterred he moves his mat and gets in my face again.

"I've already been in touch with a friend on the outside."

"And they're going to bake you a cake with pocketknife inside?"

"What are you talking about?"

"To help you break out."

Lucas shakes his head. "He can get us a car."

I freeze. What now? I was kidding. People don't escape from hospitals.

"You can get us a car?"

He points a finger at me. "Aha! That got your attention."

He's right.

"If you've got a friend who's got a car, why would you need me?"

He gets quiet. I've stumped him. Probably because ultimately, he plans to kill me and hide my body.

"Because not only do I need to get out of here. I need to get away. Figure some stuff out."

"Is this about a girl?"

I look him straight in the eyes. His pupils dilate, turning his light brown irises black before he blinks, and they reset.

"This is about me having a car and you having a destination. A plan. Am I wrong?"

"But your friend—"

I'm still not following his logic.

"Look, the doctors in cardiology said some stuff. I don't want to be around anyone I know right now. Does that make sense?"

Aha. He's in denial. Denial I get.

"So, you want to run away from your problems?" I tease. "Like Maria in the *Sound of Music*?"

He shrugs. Either he's confused or agrees. I can't tell.

"More like having nothing left to lose."

We don't exchange another word until we've rolled up our mats and stand face to face, practically eye to eye. I'm only five foot two-ish, which means he really is quite short. Muscular, but small and in proportion, like a shrunken tall guy. He could play a Marvel superhero if he were six inches taller. And older.

"Let's talk logistics. Figure out how to beat the security system." He holds up his wrist to display the hospital bracelet that can track us. "After that, first chance we get, we bolt."

I don't point out that the cake with the knife inside could have been helpful.

"We? There's no *we*."

"Sure, there is. You said 'us'."

"No, I didn't."

"Yes, you did. You said, 'He can get us a car.'"

He's right but I won't admit it.

"I barely know you. Wait, I take that back. I *don't* know you."

He looks around to make sure no one's listening.

"All the more reason to do this together," he says. "It'll keep things interesting."

"I don't want interesting. I want Normal."

"Okay, normal then. Come on, pack your bag," he says.

"I never unpacked my bag." My school backpack remains untouched, and I take what I need from the bag Dad brought me from home. Unpacking would have signaled defeat.

Chipped Tooth wags a finger at me and cocks his head. "I knew you had a plan."

By the time I find my voice, he's gone.

5

The next day, Lucas sits next to me in group. "Where're we going and when do we leave?"

"It's not that simple," I say.

"I told you. I've got someone lined up to help. Tell me what you're thinking and we'll strategize."

I want to tell him I don't have an escape plan per se. Just an idea. "Normal" used to seem like "Neverland," a fictional place with fictional directions. *Second star to the right and straight on until morning.* Until I found it on a map and some kid with a car found me. I want to tell him that I thought about it all night and for some insane reason I trust him. That I think this might work.

But my hesitation annoys him. "You know what? Forget it. I can do this alone. It'll be easier." He gets up and moves a seat away from me. I panic. I can't lose him as an ally. I glance over, but he won't look at me. He sits with his legs stretched out in front of him, arms crossed tightly across his chest.

"Lucas?" I try. But he won't budge.

"Okay, people, let's begin," says our counselor, Robert.

He makes us arrange our chairs in a circle with an empty one between us, the way Lucas and I are already sitting.

"Today we're going to give your eating disorders names," he says. "Invite he, she, or they to sit beside you."

This is off-putting on so many levels. What's the point? If there is some demon entity living inside us, do we really want to give it a name, breathe life into it? Validate it as an equal? I want to ask if we can play musical chairs instead, but I make my point a different way.

Most kids pick obvious names. Ed, Annie, Ana, Eddie, Rexie. When the group leader gets to me, I go rogue.

"Haymitch," I say.

Robert opens his mouth to say something and then decides to leave it alone. My demon. My choice.

When it's Lucas' turn he doesn't hesitate. "Foxface."

I can't believe he remembered the most minor of *Hunger Games* characters.

I cough laugh and Lucas smiles like a chipped-tooth Cheshire cat. Something inside me shifts. I threw out a line and Lucas caught it. In this room full of strangers, and their imaginary friends, we are tethered together. For once, I want to hold on.

Robert claps his hands. "Okay then. Who would like to begin the conversation with their eating disorder?"

Lucas raises his hand.

Counselor dude looks pleased. He nods toward Lucas. "Go ahead. What would you like to say to, uh—"

"Foxface," Lucas offers.

"Right. Foxface. Go ahead."

"Well, the thing is, it's not Foxface I want to talk to. It's my junior high school gym teacher. He's the guy who told me I was a pretty good wrestler for a fat kid. The one who said I was too short to be a heavy weight and too heavy to be a lightweight. He's the guy I want to talk to."

A wave of mutinous chatter makes its way around our group circle like a sped-up version of the telephone game.

Lucas stares right at me and I'm compelled to keep our very public private conversation going.

I raise my hand and speak without waiting to be acknowledged. "In fifth grade the school nurse said I was obese. She wrote the word on my height and weight chart, right next to my BMI. Then she circled it in red. Like a failing test score. I was ten."

Gemma Leonardo. *Obese. Anxious. Extra. Anorexic.* The old sticks and stones saying is wrong. Names can hurt you.

"I wonder. Would I be here right now if she'd said I was normal? I'd like to ask her about that."

It's the first true thing I've said to these people since I got here.

Lucas nods, almost imperceptibly, while the rest of the group chimes in with their own hurts.

But you have such a pretty face.

Aren't people with eating disorders supposed to be skinny?

I didn't know they made jeans in your size.

Suck in your stomach, ballet dancers don't have big bellies.

We lock eyes amidst the confusion and Lucas raises his brows.

Well? he mouths.

I'm in, I mouth back.

I wait in the hall for Lucas when group is over. I want to tell him that I'm scared, but I thought about it, and I'm ready to leave whenever he is.

But our group counselor holds him back to chat, perhaps about the kerfuffle he spurred, and I'm scheduled for a one on one with my nutritionist, who unlike my therapist, doesn't continually glance at her Apple watch and cut me off the second our session runs out of time. It'll have to wait.

Don't lose your nerve, Haymitch says.

"Shut the fuck up," I say out loud.

"See you in art tomorrow!" I call back into the room.

Lucas gives me a thumbs-up. Message received.

Later, when I return to my room, Monika is shuffling between my side of the room and hers wearing the hospital-issued grippy socks and the same sweatpants and T-shirt she's been wearing for a week.

"You're smiling," she says when she sees me.

"You're talking," I say, too shocked to stop myself.

That makes *her* smile.

"Looks good on you," she says.

"Same," I say.

Before I can say more, she's already turned her back and disappeared behind the iron curtain.

"There's an art class tomorrow if you want to go," I call to her.

To which she responds by shuffling her cards.

"I'm here if you want to talk about it," I say.

The shuffling stops, I hold my breath and wait a full thirty seconds before the fluttering of fifty-two cards begins again. At least she thought about it. Progress.

By the time I see Lucas again the following afternoon, in art therapy, I'm about to implode. I barely slept last night thinking an escape might actually be possible. He's taking supplies from the cart of the visiting artist, one whom I've never seen before. I plop down at a table near the door. Monika follows my gaze.

"Three's a crowd," she says, then drifts past me to her own table. I'm disappointed. After yesterday, I thought maybe we were getting somewhere. She tagged along with me today, albeit wordlessly, like a specter, following five feet behind without making a sound. I was hoping we could talk. That I could ask her how she's doing before she leaves for Colorado. Ever since her mother popped by to tell Monika to pack her bag for Denver, I've been even more worried about her, if that's possible.

Lucas catches my eye and I wave him over.

"Sooo," he says when he sits down across from me.

"Sooo," I echo. "Let's talk."

"Okay then. Talk."

His nonchalant, almost disinterested tone doesn't hide the fact that he's trying not to smile. I take a deep breath.

"There are five towns in the US named Normal."

Lucas rests his chin on his fist. "Go ahead, I'm listening."

I tell him about my Normal idea, unable to meet his gaze as I do. Sharing like this is hard for me, and I won't be able to stand it if he mocks me.

"Let's do it," Lucas says, slamming his palms on the table.

"Really?"

He doesn't think my idea is weird and whimsical?

"Sure. Who doesn't love a themed road trip?"

I smile, relieved that I may have found a kindred spirit.

"There will have to be rules," I say.

Am I really doing this?

"Rules. Okay. Like, what?"

I guess I am. I grab a fresh piece of art paper and start writing.

"Like the first and most important?"

1. No talking about food. *Ever.*

I look him right in the eyes.

"This includes binging, fasting, purging, excessive exercise, weird habits or rituals, and trips to the bathroom. I won't mention your puking, and you won't mention me starving. Got it?"

"Done," he says, then takes the pencil and paper and scribbles a line under mine.

2. Try not to fall in love with me.

Ugh. I snatch back the paper and pencil. "That is so cliche. A *real* rule."

"I'm serious. I don't need you getting any ideas about this being some tragic love story that ends up as a teen movie that makes girls ugly cry."

This kid. I point the eraser end of the pencil at him.

"You have absolutely nothing to worry about."

He clutches his heart in mock pain. "Ouch."

I write the next rule.

3. We don't stop until we get there.

"Where?" Lucas asks.

"Every last Normal."

"Every last Normal," he echoes, like it's our team mantra right before we break the huddle, or whatever wrestlers do before a match.

Then, in hushed tones, we start talking logistics, making lists of what we'll need.

I watch as Lucas's eyes drift behind me. Oh my God, we're busted.

I turn slowly. It's Monika, looming over me. Her long, unwashed hair brushes my shoulder as she leans down and places a folded piece of art paper in my lap. There's something heavy inside.

"Scissors," she whispers, then moves her eyes to my security bracelet.

"Thank you," I breathe. "Do you want to come?"

She shakes her head. "No, but I'll help you run."

"Tomorrow night," Lucas says. "Be ready."

I grab her wrist, so thin and fragile like a chicken bone. Frightening, not beautiful. I force her to make eye contact, so she can sense the full weight of my gratitude. She nods. I release my gentle hold and she floats away, like dandelion seeds on a puff of air.

6

The next night, a little after midnight, I'm in bed with my hands on the leads to my heart monitor, preparing to rip them loose. My resting heart rate climbs. Eighty. Ninety. Monica shuffles to my side of the room and touches my arm.

"This is it," she whispers. "We don't have much time. Here."

She hands me a card from her deck. The Joker. She has scrawled her name and number on it. "Call me. Let me know you're safe."

"Are you sure you don't want to come with us?"

Her hazel eyes soften, look rheumy behind her tears. We both know it's not possible. "I always wanted to see the Rockies. Now come on. Get up. There's only one nurse at the station. I'm going to barricade myself in a bathroom away from the elevator. Give you time."

I stand, prepare myself. Thankfully, hospital gowns aren't required, and I've been sleeping in leggings, an oversized sweatshirt, and Sherpa-lined booties since I got here. "Ah, sleeping with your boots on again. Ready to run." Spencer, one of the nurses, always says when he wakes me for weigh-ins. Bet he didn't know his joke was prescient.

Monika ducks behind the open door and lets out a banshee scream worthy of a haunted hayride or horror movie. Things move fast after that. The nurse on duty runs in. Monika runs out. It's on.

Wide-eyed, unable to release the breath I'm holding, I watch the confused nurse emerge from Monika's side of the curtain, like an actor in the wings who missed her cue. Her mouth open, she's about to ask me something, when the banshee strikes again.

"Stay away from me!" Monika's wails from somewhere farther down the hall. "No, no, no, no, no, NO!!!"

I rip the wires from my chest and run into the hallway on the nurse's heels, where I nearly crash into Lucas. We lock hands.

"Monika." It's all I can manage.

"Let's go," Lucas says.

Then we scurry back to our rooms, like two confused squirrels trying to cross the street in traffic. Grabbing my coat and backpack from the chair, I spot one of Monika's socks on the floor, scoop it up and smush it into the side water bottle pouch on my pack. I hear Lucas behind me. "Now!"

We rush into the hallway, away from Monika's screams, toward the exit. It's a Thursday night, or early Friday morning depending on how you look at it, and no one is around. Lucas slams the button on the wall to open the automatic doors. With one hand, I forage in my bag and pull out the scissors Monika stole. We duck into the stairwell, where we pause for a second to cut the bands from our wrists. Lucas is off. Taking the steps two at a time while messaging with one hand on a phone. My backpack weighs me down. My feet and my thoughts can't keep up.

"Wait." My lungs burn and I'm light-headed. This is all happening sooner than I expected.

Lucas slows down but doesn't stop. "Give me your bag," he says. I shake my head and try to move faster.

"They let you keep your phone?" I ask through choppy breaths.

"No one checked my bag when I transferred in from cardiology."

Lucky.

"Come on. We gotta move."

I follow as fast as I can, uncertain I'll make it without keeling over and dying.

When we reach the ground floor, I fold over, hands on my knees, heart pumping like hummingbird wings. Monika's face dances before me. *I've always wanted to see the Rockies.* That's what she said, and I hope it's code for she wants to get better.

"Why do I get the feeling you've done stuff like this before?" I choke out, breathless when we reach the ground floor.

"Told you. I've had lots of practice staying two or three moves ahead of my opponents."

Lucas grabs my wrist and pulls me out the exit door and into the raw October night. I inhale the crisp air, grateful for its freshness. I've been sequestered on the adolescent med floor for weeks, missing the scent of falling leaves, woodburning stoves, and…chocolate. I forgot how close we are to Hershey Park. Mmm. Chocolate air. My dream dessert.

Lucas glances at his phone, then looks both ways before deciding where we should go next. "This way." Lucas points toward a deserted service road and we both begin running again. It feels like a familiar nightmare, where the bad guys are chasing me, and my legs are like lead.

We finally make it to a riverfront park and slow down as we approach a footbridge spanning the Susquehanna River. The full moon hangs high in the sky, swathing the riverbank in light. Lucas and I stick to the shadows.

"Almost there." Lucas breathes heavily now too. "Declan's meeting us on the other side."

"Declan?"

"My friend and teammate."

We step onto the footbridge. Wind rushes above and below us as we make our way across. Bone cold, I stuff numb hands into my pockets, wishing I remembered to pack a hat and gloves. My nose and cheeks have lost all feeling.

Another park, a mirror-image to the one we left behind, awaits us on the other side. So does a tall, imposing figure in a green army jacket and black wool beanie.

Declan, I presume. He puts one hand up, like he's hailing a taxi. As if we'd confuse him with some other person waiting by a river in the middle of the night to pick up two hospital freaks.

"S'up?" he says and gives Lucas a bro hug that envelops my diminutive new friend.

"Thanks for coming, man," Lucas says.

Declan sort of grunts an answer then turns toward me. "You the girl who ruined my weekend plans?"

If I thought Lucas was the kind of overconfident jock who never looked my way in high school, this guy is that times ten. I decide to hate him.

I give him the finger.

He sees me now.

In his hard stare, I imagine he's doing a mental scroll through all the beautiful girls who've fallen for his jacked-up body and seeing how I match up. I already regret leaving the hospital to face real-world judgment. What I wouldn't give to be a Declan instead of a Gemma.

"You're very cold. Come on. My truck's this way."

His double-entendre notwithstanding I'm grateful for the toasty warmth as I slip into the backseat and begin to thaw. His truck smells guy-ish. Gym bag meets cologne. My latent hormones kick into high gear. I tell them to calm the fuck down and not get all worked up over this asshole.

I buckle my seatbelt and cross my arms over my chest, uncomfortable with the way it separates my boobs and the fact that there are boobs to separate. The truck engine rumbles to life, the blaring car stereo with it.

"Sorry," Declan says.

He turns it down and whisks us into the night like he's part of a Navy SEAL extraction team. I turn to Lucas.

"Uh, where are we going?" I ask.

Is Declan going with us? I ask him with my eyes and a quick nod of my head.

"Dillsburg," Lucas says. "You and I will leave from there."

I relax.

"There's a town called Dillsburg?" I ask.

"Home of Mr. Pickle," Declan says. "We drop him down a pole every New Year's Eve."

I turn to Lucas. "He's kidding."

Lucas twists to face me. "Oh, how I wish he were. I've been going to the annual pickle drop for as long as I can remember. You should come this year. If you don't have better plans."

He stares at me like he's actually waiting for an answer. It dawns on me that Lucas doesn't know I live in New Jersey, not central Pennsylvania. Before I can explain, or maybe because I don't, Lucas turns his attention to Declan. "Thanks for doing this, bro. I owe you big. Were you able to get some of my requests?"

"Water, sustenance, and a burner phone are in that bag near your feet. Don't call me or anyone else. For emergencies only. It can probably be traced."

"Cash?" Lucas asks.

Declan nods. "Everything you asked for plus what I owed you."

Lucas and I estimated how much gas money we'd need for a 2,000-mile trip.

"Thanks, man. I'll pay you back," Lucas says.

"I know where you live. Camping gear and costumes are in the back."

"Costumes? Like for Halloween?" I ask.

"It *is* in three days," Lucas reminds me. "On Sunday."

Halloween is this Sunday? Hospital days and nights bleed together. Dead hours, lost time, dread for the coming week. That's been my life for the past month. And now the early decision deadline for college admissions is fast approaching. Dad wanted me to hold off making that kind of commitment, but I need to know sooner rather than later that my four-year sentence in high school is over and I can begin again where no one knows me. It's the only way I will get better.

"I should have said *disguises*. Eventually you two will get reported as missing or runaways and there are security cams everywhere," Declan says.

"It's true," Lucas says. "Fugitives always get spotted at convenience stores."

Or no-tell motels frequented by drug dealers and adulterers. Guess that's why Declan brought camping gear. I was so focused on escaping, I failed to consider the details from this point on.

"What kind of disguises?" I ask.

"A couple of my sister's wigs for you. Shades and a baseball cap for this guy."

"Wait, no fake mustache or goatee?" Lucas says.

"Dude. You have skin like a baby's ass. You couldn't pull off facial hair."

Lucas's cheeks flush. Instinctively I rush to protect Lucas from this alpha male.

"So, which one of you has the better record? Is that what you call it? In wrestling?"

I already know Lucas has never lost a match.

"Me," Lucas says without hesitation. "Last year I was undefeated."

"As a lightweight," Declan clarifies.

"Undefeated is undefeated, right?" I say. "No need to make the lightweight feel small."

Declan turns up the music again. I smile to myself and sink into the song, letting it lull me with a comforting heaviness as the city lights fade behind us, turning the back seat into a dark, cozy cave. My eyes keep closing involuntarily. I struggle to snap them open again.

Before long, Declan makes a turn into an industrial park. The street dead-ends at a junkyard.

Dillsburg Auto Salvage Inc. says the hand-painted sign on the fence.

"Wait here," Declan says.

Cold air rushes in as Declan gets out and jogs toward the fifteen-foot chain-link fence. The dashboard chimes incessantly. Declan removes the padlock and rolls open the gate before returning to the truck.

"What are we doing here?" I ask.

"My father owns the place."

Gravel crunches beneath the tires as we roll through the gate and between rows and rows of junk cars, hubcaps, mufflers, engines. It's like we've arrived at the end of the world and everything's in pieces.

Finally, he parks and turns off the truck. "Let's go. It's right over here," he says.

"What is?" I ask.

"Your getaway car?"

I scowl at the "duh" in Declan's voice.

Why did I think *this* was our getaway car? At what point did I cede my destiny to these two strangers from Dillsburg, Pennsylvania? They could kill me right now and bury me under old tires. My recklessness makes my pulse quicken and yet here I am, padding after Declan and Lucas like a baby duck. A baby goose. A stupid, silly goose.

"What do you think?" Declan says as we round a corner.

That I'm unmoored, floating high above my well-ordered life, farther away from "Normal" than I've ever been. That there's a high level of probability that this will all end badly. Like drive-off-a-cliff-into-the-Grand-Canyon badly with no one to kiss me goodbye. How did I get here? I want to scream. But I give myself a mental slap, allow my eyes to adjust to the darkness, and focus on the less existential question regarding the car.

"That's a shit ton of metal," I say.

7

A four-door behemoth, mostly blue with big grayish splotches, sits beside a cinder block garage. It reminds me of these giant fish called Oscars at the pet store where I worked this past summer. They get ugly spots on their scales when they contract this fungus called Ick. The name says it all. I have to drop Tetracycline in the tank when that happens.

"What kind of car is that?" Lucas asks.

"Chevy Impala. 1978 or '79," I say. Declan and Lucas both look at me. "My dad's a mechanic. Identifying cars was a game we played during long car trips. Punch buggy and the license plate game were too pedestrian for him."

Dad was always dragging me to Friday night car shows in the Target parking lot. I know all the gems, '57 Chevies, '66 Mustangs, and '69 GTOs. Dad's favorites are older than him.

Declan nods. "My dad and I spent the last year rebuilding the engine. It stays locked up here in one of the garages. He won't miss it until Monday, the earliest."

"V8?" I ask.

A gas guzzler. I'm suddenly worried about having enough money.

Declan dangles the keys in front of me. "Yep. Lots of pick up. Sure you can handle it?"

Worried morphs to terrified. Wait a min—

"Me?"

I've barely driven at all since getting my license. Panic takes hold, wrenching the air from my lungs. I'm not sure about anything. Least of all, driving this tugboat. I shake my head looking from Declan to Lucas, who shrugs.

"There's no way I can drive this thing on the highway." My voice quavers.

"We should probably stick to backroads for a while, anyway," Lucas says.

"Why don't you drive?"

"Can't. I'm not old enough."

His words knock me back. I lean my butt against the car door. What the hell, Lucas? This is exactly why I prefer to work solo. Alone may be lonely, but it's safe.

"How old are you anyway?"

"Sixteen in December."

He's fifteen? Cue the Taylor Swift song.

"You didn't need my plan. You needed a babysitter," I spit out. It's the fear talking, but still.

"And you needed a car," Lucas shoots back.

That shuts me up. He's right of course. But I'm not backing down. We glare at each other until Lucas jams his hands in his front pockets and looks down at his black Converse. Small victory but I'll take it. When he looks up again, he takes a tentative step toward me. "Look, maybe I should've—"

I take the keys from Declan's hand. "Forget it. I got it."

I don't got it. I really don't.

Declan laughs and puts a hand on Lucas' shoulder. "Come on, junior. Help me transfer the gear from my truck to the car. Give her space before she rips your balls off."

While Declan and Lucas load the trunk—you could fit three or four dead bodies in there—I sit behind the wheel to familiarize myself with the gauges. I find the wipers, the temperature control, blinkers, and emergency flashers, then adjust the mirrors. The gear shift is actually on the steering column. No console in the middle, just one long bench seat. Nothing electronic or automatic. The radio has dials and knobs with a trap door underneath that looks like a mail slot. I take a deep breath. It smells like an old leather bag that got left out in the rain.

When they're done packing up, Lucas slips into the passenger side—he's like four feet away from me on the black leather seat—and holds up his phone. "Got anyone you want to call before we go off the grid?"

I'm still pissed, but I'm always pissed. I can't blame Lucas for that. I think of Dad. I'm desperate to tell him I'm okay, but if I hear his voice, I'll lose my nerve. I take the phone and dial my gram—the last person on the planet with a physical answering machine and no call waiting. She's been asleep for hours. I leave a rambling message, telling her I'm fine, that I'll call again soon, that the hospital was getting to me.

"I needed a break. Please, please, please tell Dad I love him and that I'm safe and with a friend. Love you. Bye."

My voice cracks. I've spent my entire life ping-ponging between two spots. Home to school. School to home. Home to the library. Library to home. There has never been a time when my dad didn't know where I was going, when I would get there, and when I'd be home. When he couldn't watch my dot moving on his smartphone.

I hand the phone back to Lucas. "Did you call your parents?"

"Dec will text them from my phone in an hour. Buy us some time."

I start the car and give it some gas. An hour. We'll still be in Pennsylvania in an hour.

Declan taps on my window, motions to the door panel, and makes a turning motion. I crank the handle and the window inches down. Declan bends down and looks around me at Lucas.

"Phone?"

Lucas hands his cell to me. I pass it to Declan, then lean back so Lucas can see his face.

"When you leave town, drive that in the opposite direction from where we're headed," Lucas says.

"Which is?"

"South," I say.

"West," Lucas says.

"Southwest," I clarify. "Kentucky."

"What's in Kentucky?"

Horseracing. Moonshine. Coal.

"Nothing," I say.

"Normal," Lucas says.

I shoot him a look. *Seriously?*

What? Lucas's eyes say.

Declan puts up his hands in surrender. "Probably better if I don't know. Plausible deniability and all that." He looks at Lucas. "What about Kaitlin? The four of us were supposed—"

My ears perk up.

"Tell her I want my jacket back," Lucas says.

I notice for the first time that Lucas is wearing a too-big maroon wrestling sweatshirt with the name *Nick* stitched in gray thread over his left pec. Who the hell is Nick and why is Lucas wearing his sweatshirt? I picture Kaitlin warming her bony ass in Lucas's varsity jacket. High school tropes aside, I envy this girl for the coverage and cache a jacket like that can give her.

"That's cold, bro," Declan says.

"Uh, speaking of cold. Does this car have heat?" I ask. My cheeks are frozen.

"Sort of." Declan takes off his gloves and passes them through the window. "Here."

I slip them on without arguing. They fit like Mickey Mouse hands. Who cares that I'm a sellout, accepting gifts and feeding his ego? They're sooo warm. "Thank you," I breathe.

Declan waves me off.

"I don't need you crashing my car because your hands were frozen. Better get out of here before people come looking."

People will come looking. When they don't locate us in the hospital, they'll call our parents, who will call the local police. It won't be long before they track Lucas's phone to Dillsburg and Declan.

"Where's the nearest bus station?" I ask.

"Are you insane? We're not taking a bus." Lucas is freaking.

"Oh my God, will you relax. I was thinking that's where Declan should take your phone. He can text your parents from there, then turn off all cellular and Wi-Fi connections or whatever so it can't be tracked."

Lucas looks like he's about to say something, but Declan

cuts him off. "No, bro. That works. They'll think you took a bus and leave me out of it."

Lucas nods. "Okay, yeah. That's kinda genius."

"I spend a lot of Friday nights watching true crime."

I roll up the window. Declan flashes the peace sign then pats the roof twice.

Godspeed, his lips say through the glass.

I put the car in drive and pull away.

8

Maneuvering this hulking tank through the front gate proves to be like threading a needle with a cherry Twizzler. When I ding the side-view mirror on the fence Lucas winces but says not to worry because the car needs a paint job anyway.

"With all these spots. It looks like it has a sexually transmitted disease," he says.

"Or Ick," I offer. "Like *Ichthyophthirius multifili*. It's a disease freshwater fish get. Technically it's 'Ich.' But all the treatments we sell say 'Ick' on package. So—"

Lucas's expression stops me.

"What? I worked in a pet store this summer."

"Clearly," he says. "When you weren't watching true crime."

We fall into a silence after that, the headlights pushing through the darkness as I navigate the Impala down a two-lane county road. This car. It's so heavy and there's so much bulk to it that outside seems far away. It's like we're trapped behind impenetrable walls, subsumed by a giant cellular organism that's eating us. What's that called again?

"Phagocytosis," I mumble.

"Huh?"

I glance at Lucas. Poor bastard doesn't know he's being digested.

Then weirdly, for the first time in a long time, anticipation replaces fear. Back when we took family road trips, we always left in the middle of the night. I'd sleep in comfortable clothes, the car packed and waiting in the driveway. Mom would nudge me awake and I'd take my pillow and blanket into the Honda's backseat and immediately fall back to sleep. By the time I woke, we'd be ready for our first pit stop and breakfast. Egg

McMuffins were my favorite back when I had favorite foods and wasn't afraid to eat them.

But tonight, I'm the driver. Wide awake and staring down the highway entrance ramp looming up ahead. Morning, breakfast sandwiches, and anyone who loves me are all very far away. I press the gas and feel this hulking monstrosity accelerate beneath us like a charging bull, prompting me to scooch closer to the steering wheel to get a better grip while praying it doesn't get away from me as I merge onto the interstate.

The blaring horn of a semi knocks the breath out of me as it quickly changes lanes to avoid rear-ending us.

Lucas tilts his head and cracks his neck, a nervous tick I first noticed back in the hospital.

"Give it some gas," Lucas says, and I obey.

Thankfully, there aren't too many cars on the road this time of night.

"You're doing great," he says.

"Am I? Am I really doing great? Because it feels like we're Luke and Leia stuck in the Death Star garbage compactor and the walls are closing in. You know, you took a big risk assuming I had a license. I almost bailed on my road test."

"What do you take me for? I'm a wrestler. We have back-up plans for our back-up plans. Counter moves to avoid being pinned. I would have figured something out."

Lucas begins fumbling with the radio dials before I have a chance to ask him to elaborate. I know absolutely nothing about wrestling.

"Okay, so would you rather—"

I cut Lucas off. "Oh no, no, no. We're not doing this. No Truth or Dare or would you rather games."

"That wasn't in the rules."

"I don't care. I'm not playing."

"Why?"

Why? Because my lack of life experience is cringy. I never drank cheap beer out of big red cups or made out with someone under the high school bleachers. I don't do group chats or sleepovers or anything else that requires me to put too much of myself out there.

"Because. I would prefer not to."

"Okay then, who's your favorite president?"

I huff. "So now we're going to do twenty questions?"

"One question. We're doing one question," Lucas says.

"William Henry Harrison."

"What? He's no one's favorite president."

"He's mine," I say.

"He was only president for, like, a month."

"Thirty-one days. He died of pneumonia after standing outside in the cold without a hat or coat delivering the longest inaugural address in history."

"And that makes him your favorite president because…" Lucas says.

"I admire that kind of stubbornness."

"You're confounding, Gemma Leonardo."

I smile. "Just like William Henry Harrison."

"And Bartleby. Thought you could slip that reference by me without me noticing." Lucas taps to his temple. "Wrestlers. Good brains."

The distraction from the highway of doom stretching before us is short-lived. My eyes keep getting drawn to the rubber skid marks veering off the road in various patterns and directions, remnants of horrific traffic accidents I can't help picturing in graphic detail. My palms are sweating in Declan's gloves. I shake one off then the other. Lucas furrows his brow.

"Do you think that was deer blood or human blood back there in the road?"

"Music might help," he says.

There's nothing but static and talk radio as a red line moves between a five and eight, ten, thirteen and sixteen, on what looks like an unevenly spaced ruler. What do those numbers even mean? I tighten my grip on the steering wheel, dig my thumbnails into the faux leather.

"Turn it off. Just turn it off."

"Okay, okay." Desperate, Lucas fumbles with the glove compartment door, eventually prying it open. "What the fuck?"

"What? What is it? I think I need to pull over."

"Relax, breathe." He waves a chunky cartridge around. "It's just Kool and the Gang. Celebrate!"

"Celebrate what?"

"It's their big hit from the '80s. The title track? You know, celebrate good times, come on."

"Please don't sing."

"You've seriously never heard this song? Have you never been to a wedding or bat mitzvah? I wonder if this thing works."

Before I can answer or stop him, Lucas inserts the oversized cassette in the radio mail slot and after a few uncertain seconds of listening to the tape scratch along, there's a funky musical explosion of drums, guitar, horns, backup singers and—

"Wahoo!"

Lucas. I jump so high my ass cheeks leave the seat and the tires hit the rumble strips on the shoulder, which makes me jump again. My embarrassment for him is going to get us killed.

"Uh, what else is in there?" I ask, hoping to refocus him so he'll stop pumping his fist.

"Queen's Greatest Hits, Boston, The Bee Gees, and Billy Joel. Makes you wonder who exactly owned this car? Disco queen? Drag queen?"

A quick flash. A micro memory. Windows down, the car carrying us down some highway. Mom singing. Dad and I joining her for the chorus.

"What?" Lucas's tone tells me the look on my face is cause for concern.

I shake my head. "Nothing. My mom loved Billy Joel."

Lucas looks straight ahead, nods knowingly, and does the neck crack thing again. "I didn't know—"

"Lucas, don't worry about it. How could you know? I don't go around saying, 'Hello, my name is Gemma. My mom is dead.'"

Though I wish I had during that first session with Dr. Paige

"Fucking" Bryant. She was prying into my mom's medical history, wanting to know if she suffered from anxiety, OCD, or some other mental illness.

Every mom gives her kids something, she said on my first day inpatient.

I wanted to punch her in the neck. I wonder what she'll give *her* kids someday. Her insipid cache of go-to phrases? Her undivided attention for only fifty minutes each day, until the timer goes off? I'll bet Paige Fucking Bryant would have no clue what to do with a kid like me.

I say to Lucas now what I should have said to my stupid shrink back then.

"For the record, I don't have dead mommy issues, okay? She died from an autoimmune disease, like Lupus, only rarer and less understood. I miss her every day but my shit is my shit. End of story. I was bigger and wanted to be smaller. Is that so hard for people to understand? Skinny equals better, isn't that the message that gets jammed down our throats from everyone?"

Without asking, he ejects Kool and the Gang and puts in Billy Joel.

"Track two was her favorite. She could play it on piano."

"'Summer, Highland Falls,' huh? I like a song title that makes use of punctuation."

Of course, he does.

"It's about manic depression. Bipolar disorder."

"Even better," Lucas says.

I can see her at the upright in our living room, fingers running back and forth, playing these finger-twisting arpeggios. The piano is a silent piece of furniture now, sitting untouched like a stone sarcophagus that holds my parents' wedding photo, my framed school pictures, and Mom's ashes.

"Do you play?" Lucas asks.

"She tried to teach me, but I'm musically challenged."

"Same."

At least he admits it.

Lucas was right, the music distracts me. My muscles relax and I loosen the death grip I have on the steering wheel.

My mind stops seeing the road stretching out ahead as memories unfold like paper maps with well-worn creases that sometimes make each opening and closing easier, sometimes not. Sometimes the pages get rearranged and tucked away with roads and highways that weren't supposed to touch and so they lay atop one another until we reopen it, shake it out, lay it flat, smooth it with our palm, and retrace the dots and lines that led us through time to this point.

When the album's done, Lucas pops out the 8-Track and returns it to the glove compartment.

"Take this next exit. We can ride the backroads beside the interstate for a while," he says.

I do as he says. The two-lane county road is a welcome reprieve.

"So my dad's been out of work for more than a year now," he says after we've been driving in silence for a few miles.

"Lucas, that's sucks. I'm sorry."

"Don't be. He'll either find work or he won't. But until then, my parents are blowing through their small savings. I might not get medical clearance after being in the hospital and I need a wrestling scholarship. Even though I'm their only kid, they'll never be able to help out with college."

Huh. Lucas is an Only, like me. Though Dad likes to call me "The One" because it doesn't rhyme with "lonely."

"There's all kinds of ways beside sports scholarships to pay for college."

"I know. I don't want you feeling sorry for me or anything. It's not about the money so much. It's more like my dad looks forward to wrestling season as much as I do. Maybe more. It's our common ground. If he's not working and I'm not wrestling…" He pauses, clears his throat. "I'm not sure what we'll have to talk about. I can't face that silence."

It wasn't only about my driver's license.

I nod. "I get it."

I don't remember the last time my dad and I talked about anything other than food.

Want me to pick you up anything from the store?

No.

Did you eat lunch today?

Yes.

Baby girl, I don't understand. Why won't you just eat on your own?

Silence

Well then, you'll have to stay here until you do.

"I told my father I hated him the last time he visited," I say to Lucas now. "I wanted him to sign me out and he wouldn't."

"And so here we are."

On our way to Normal, suspended in that space in between. One provided by four car doors, an ancient 8-Track stereo, and expansive leather seats. We both need this. I'm about to say as much to Lucas, when I spot something in the road, a turtle-like lump, or rock. Instead of maneuvering around it, I slam the brake with both feet. Lucas and I lurch forward, then fall back against the bench seat in unison as we skid to a rubber-burning halt. A tiny creature tries to walk, wobbles, falls flat on its belly, motionless. I throw the car into park and swing the door open.

"What are you doing? We're in the middle of the road."

"Right. Flashers." I flip on the emergency lights and jump out to investigate.

9

Kitten?

No. Kit.

A baby racoon. Weeks old from the looks of him. With a faint black mask circling his closed eyes and tiny bandit-like "hands," perfect for lifting up garbage can lids or peeling an orange.

Its tiny chest heaves up and down. He's alive. Thank goodness. The tightness around my own heart loosens as I scoop up the tiny nugget with my gloved hands. It's like holding air.

I look around.

"Did you lose your momma, little man? What about your brothers and sisters?"

My breath puffs warm white clouds into the cold.

I squint into the darkness. Where there's one baby, there should be more. Unless he's another Only, like me and Lucas, which, unless we're talking baby elephants, would be unusual. Handling wild baby animals is generally a no-no, but seeing as we're in the middle of the road and all, what else can I do? Plop him along the roadside and hope for the best?

I walk along the shoulder, scanning the brush along the tree line. The smell of pine and falling leaves triggers images of Thanksgiving, fall break, big family dinners. Food. Why must it always be right there, so close to the surface, clouding my thoughts and punctuating every minute of every day? I hum to myself, the song about three little birds and everything being all right, and keep walking until thoughts of mashed potatoes and pumpkin pie with whipped cream abate. Holidays would be more enjoyable without the feeding frenzies. And Mom's empty chair, of course.

A few yards away, a gray and black lump, with a defining black and gray candy-striped tail, comes into focus. It's splayed out on the roadside, innards spilling onto the pavement. I gag but don't stop my approach. I hate what I'm about to do, but sense I need to. I know that when families with multiple pets need to send one fur baby over the rainbow bridge, it helps to eliminate confusion if the other pets are present. I squat beside the raccoon carcass and hold the baby close. His wet black nose twitches, his eyes stay closed.

"Looks like you and me got something in common, huh?"

Headlights pass over us and I stand up shielding my eyes.

"What are you doing? Get in the car!" Lucas yells.

He pulls the Impala beside me and is now glaring through the open passenger door window. What the?

"What am I doing? What are *you* doing?"

I walk around the car and yank open the passenger door with an exaggerated huff and slide in.

"I thought you couldn't drive," I say.

"I never said that. I've been driving around my uncle's farm since I was twelve. I just don't have my license yet and—"

Lucas watches me click my seat belt and make myself comfortable.

"What are you doing?"

"Holding a baby raccoon while you drive," I say.

"Uh yeah. Got that first part. But I can't drive without a license. If we get pulled over, that's it. Trip's over and I'll be registering for selective service before I get a license."

"Both of us are already in trouble. This car doesn't even belong to us. Are the plates valid? Is it registered? Insured?"

Lucas looks like he's never considered these questions. "So?"

"So, drive or take care of Chester. Your choice." The name pops straight from the pages of a favorite children's book. *The Kissing Hand.* It was everything when I was five. That and the heartwarming tale *Germs Make Me Sick.* I couldn't get enough.

"Chester? You've already named it?"

"Him. I've named him."

"How do you know it's a boy?"

"Because he has little—"

"Don't call it little. You'll give him a complex."

I hold Chester closer to my mouth and whisper to him. "Hear that, Chester. Lucas is already being protective of your manhood."

Lucas grimaces.

"Don't get so close! What if he has rabies or worms or fleas? Or some other disgusting raccoon disease? They kill cats you know. What if he bites you and you foam at the mouth and I have to put you down like a rabid dog?"

"He looks fine."

I hold Chester under his front legs and dangle him in Lucas' face. The bitty bandit yawns and curls his tongue back to reveal a couple of miniscule teeth.

"I mean it. I would hate to shoot you."

"His mother is dead."

Yes. I'm going there.

"Yes, I gathered when I saw you paying your last respects."

"I was giving Chester closure. If we leave him here, he'll starve."

The word tumbles out of my mouth before I can catch it and its irony.

Lucas sighs. "Fine. But when we get closer to civilization, you take the wheel in case we get pulled over."

"If the police pull us over, we'll have bigger things to worry about."

"Like illegal raccoon possession?" Lucas asks.

"Like grand theft auto?"

"We're borrowing a car."

"Right. The perfect legal defense."

Lucas groans, cracks his neck, and puts the car in gear.

"Don't get too comfortable, furball. First chance we get we're finding you a new home," he says as he pulls onto the dark road. Empty, except for Chester's broken mommy.

10

We opt to stay off the interstate now that Lucas is behind the wheel. I navigate the backroads while he drives.

"My mom used to read me this book called *The Kissing Hand*," I say when the car gets too quiet. "It's about this raccoon who's afraid to go to kindergarten, so his mother presses her nose into his hand and he transfers her 'kiss' to his cheek."

I demonstrate with my own hand.

"We're talking about Chester, I assume," Lucas says.

I nod. "The kissing hand is like an imprint. A way to carry his mom with him forever."

In nature, imprints are like invisible tattoos. Indelible, olfactory signals forever linking a mother and child. That kind of bond might be bigger than love because it's biological. Tangible.

At the risk of sounding weird or overly sentimental, I proceed to tell Lucas how the book helped me overcome my own fear of kindergarten.

"My mom would spritz her perfume on a Post-it, and I'd tuck it in a pocket or my lunch box so she always felt close by."

"Smell is the sense most closely linked to memory," he says.

"I know. My dad got rid of all Mom's stuff before I realized I'd want to keep something that smelled like her. Hand lotion, clothes, her perfume. Anything that could have kept her with me longer."

Lucas nods. "Do you remember what kind of perfume she wore? I know it wouldn't be hers, per se, but—"

He trails off, leaving me to wonder why I never thought to ask my dad. It's only recently that I've begun to apply adult logic to my kid trauma. Mom had scleroderma, an obscure name for an obscure disease, which made it harder for me to process and explain to the kids in my school. Of course, scleroderma has been easy enough to research as I got older, though its cause seems to remain a medical mystery.

What I've really come to understand, and to dwell on in recent weeks, is that her body turned on her. The system meant to protect her from disease, became the disease, attacking healthy cells and tissue and ultimately shutting down her lungs and heart. It's not genetic, I've learned, but in my own mind the part about the body's betrayal is.

The car is quiet, not uncomfortably so, but enough to amplify the absurdity of my current situation, driving through the night in a borrowed car, with a boy I've only recently met and a baby raccoon who may or may not wake up and sink his rabid teeth into my flesh.

I open the glove box and pop in another 8-Track, Queen this time, and let Freddie Mercury rock us for the next hour as we drive toward the blood red orange sky of morning. If I were at the hospital right now, I'd be stepping backward on a scale (we're not allowed to know our weight) with only a bra, panties, and an empty bladder under my hospital gown. Being free of the demoralizing ritual for the first time in some twenty-odd days buoys my mood.

Chester is curled up on my thighs, his tiny heart thrumming in double-time as he sleeps with his head resting on his paws. I wish I had my phone. These are the kinds of moments social media is good for. I crane my neck toward the gauges in front of Lucas.

"How're we doing on gas? We should find someplace to stop. Switch drivers. Stretch our legs," I say.

"Maybe get something to—" Lucas catches himself. "I really need to pee."

"I haven't had caffeine in a month and I'm dying for coffee."

"I wasn't sure if—"

"It's fine."

"In that case, can you pass that bag at your feet?"

I hand it to him, and he fishes around inside until he pulls out a protein bar, which he opens with his teeth. My stomach growls, rousing Chester, who stirs and resettles himself on my lap. Lucas gives us both a sidelong glance.

"What do baby raccoons eat?" Lucas asks through a mouthful.

I hate the sound of chewing and swallowing, and Lucas is particularly loud.

"Mother's milk. But maybe kitten formula would be okay. We sold it at the pet store where I worked."

Lucas chews his protein bar and looks at Chester, concerned. I read his mind.

"I know, I know. He complicates things."

"Yeah, like, where's it going to shit?" Lucas asks.

"We'll have to get a box or something. Train it to use kitty litter. I don't know. I wasn't planning on finding a baby raccoon."

"Does anyone plan to find a baby raccoon? Does anyone even notice a baby raccoon? Chester would have been roadkill if I'd been driving," Lucas says.

I stroke the area between Chester's eyes with my thumb.

"Exactly. I can't help it. I love animals and the only pets I've ever had were tropical fish and the African dwarf frog they let me take home in fifth grade after we finished our science project. Munchkin. He lived for five years."

Lucas smirks.

"What?" I'm defensive.

"Nothing. Just wondering what you do for fun."

"Homework."

"Homework isn't fun."

"No, it really isn't. But it's what I've got."

"What about movies, coffee shops, drinking in the woods?"

I roll my eyes at the last one. "You know those kids you see at school dances and parties hanging on the fringes looking awkward?"

"Don't tell me you're one of those."

"Worse. I'm the girl no one invited."

I didn't mean to go full-on Eeyore on him, but it's true. No one ever asks me to do anything.

"Bullshit."

I bristle at Lucas's angry tone and assume an internal fight stance. "Excuse me?"

"You heard me. I said *bullshit*. You're the girl who doesn't look up from her AP study guides long enough to notice when she's been invited."

"What are you talking about?"

"Uh, let's see. For starters, this whole trip"

Lucas seems genuinely pissed and I don't like it. He has no idea what school is like for me. How I walk the halls like a skittish cat, afraid of walking into a classroom, or to my locker, or God forbid the cafeteria, and have someone make fun of me. First for being fat, then for being too smart. I'm always too much of one thing and not enough of whatever it is that's supposed to make people like me. It's exhausting, hiding in plain sight from the packs of laughing hyenas who troll the high school halls on the daily.

"And back in Dillsburg? At the junkyard?"

Oh, for fuck's sake, is he still on this?

"I asked you to come watch the pickle drop with us on New Year's."

I think back to our brief pickle conversation.

"No. You didn't."

"Not outright, because to be honest, you kind of scare me. But I strongly hinted that it would be cool to have you there. And then there's Declan. Don't get me started. I've never seen somebody so impervious to his charms."

"Charms? Really? Maybe he would have kicked it up a notch if I still had big tits." I choke on a laugh.

"He gave you his gloves!"

Oh, come on. He's the kind of guy who wants his girlfriend to eat hamburgers and fries in front of him without gaining an ounce. The kind that respects her virginity as long as she doesn't mind giving him blow jobs. Anyway. Even if what Lucas says is true, Declan's flirting was most likely an alpha dog move to one-up Lucas, again.

"Sounds like your problem is with Declan, not me." I close one eye and brace myself for the neck crack.

"He looks out for me. Without Declan and wrestling I'd be a social pariah," Lucas says.

"So he's your manic pixie dream boy," I say.

"My what?"

"Your foil. Your 'Mr. My Only Life Goal is To Help you Find Yours.' Mary Poppins, Star Girl, Penny Lane. Don Quixote's Dulcinea. The Manic Pixie Dream Girl has been a trope in the arts for centuries."

"Your cynicism in the human race runs deep, Leonardo. How do you know I'm not *your* Manic Pixie Dream Boy?"

"I—"

He's not. He can't be. We ran away to save ourselves, not each other. I reach over and pinch his arm.

"Ouch!" Lucas rubs his arm.

"Sorry! You didn't pass the pixie pinch test," I say.

"Now you're just making shit up. And you're wrong about Dec. He's my best friend. I've got his back. He's got mine. Chess club. Debate team. We're the same. Except he's a heavyweight."

I can bet that one exception is the one that matters to Lucas most.

"Bet your GPA is higher," I say.

"Dec's smart. He had a rough go of it the past few years and had to catch up. I tutored him in pre-calc. Wrote a few papers for him."

"Is that why he owes you money?"

His silence is answer enough.

"Enough about Declan already. Tell me about Mr. Pickle," I say.

The chipped tooth reappears as he smiles. "He's quite phallic if you must know. Like a green uncircumcised penis in a top hat sliding down a pole."

I burst out laughing, which makes Lucas laugh too.

"A penis pickle pole dance? I'm in," I say.

"There's a Mrs. Pickle too. And pickle soup," he says.

I can't tell if he's being ironic or immature.

"No need to oversell it. If you'd been more direct the first time, I would have told you I live more than three hours away. In New Jersey. Sorry if you thought I blew you off."

"Jersey? Now I'm sorry."

"Watch it, pickle boy."

"Hey, I'm Dillsburg proud."

"And I'm Nutley proud."

His eyes get wide. "Seriously? You live in a town called Nutley and I'm not supposed to joke about that?"

I fake growl.

"The point is, I live eight miles outside of New York City. Kind of far to drive for New Year's."

"Okay, okay. That complicates things. I thought you were local. Maybe you could bring a friend?"

"Who is this fictitious friend you speak of? Did you not hear me?"

"You can stay at my house. Unless that would be too weird. Would that be too weird?"

It would. But I lie.

"It wouldn't be too weird. But I'm not eating pickle soup."

No harm in making fake plans, right?

"Noted."

"And what about Kaitlin?"

He grimaces and cracks his neck. Should have seen that coming. "You mean the reason I'm wearing a sweatshirt from the school lost and found? She'll get over it."

"Well, thank God you cleared that up because I did not want to spend the next one hundred miles wondering who Nick was. Now find me coffee before I die."

11

U h. This is sooo good." I sip my coffee and sigh. Though I have no firsthand experience for comparison, I'm fairly certain my extra-large dark roast coffee with stevia and almond milk is better than sex.

There's no place to put my coffee while I drive. Apparently, cigarette lighters and ashtrays had priority over cup holders in 1979. So we're sitting in the parking lot while I finish.

"Do you two want to be alone?" Lucas asks.

"Shut. It," I snap.

Here on the backroads, there are no fancy rest stops with food courts and trendy lattes with fake Italian names. But the guy working the overnight shift at Go Mart was kind enough to make me a fresh pot of coffee and let me use his cell phone. I appreciate that Elden, according to his name tag, knows the value of a fresh brew and has a calling plan with unlimited minutes. I wanted to hug him or at least high five him. Instead, like a vampire needing a fix, I sucked down my first cup right there at the counter then got myself this extra-large cup to go.

I shoot a sideways glance at Lucas, who's sitting in the passenger seat, as I study my road map and guzzle what's left of my second cup. He's holding a shitload of fat and calories disguised as an innocuous breakfast sandwich in waxy yellow paper.

"You know that came from a gas station convenience store, right?"

That's what my mouth says. My eyes say, *How long until you puke it up?*

Lucas is nonplussed. "Perhaps the better question might be, How much coffee can the human bladder really hold?"

Why aren't you hungry? his eyes ask.

I *am* hungry, but ignoring my stomach's roiling gastric juices is my superpower. I hear the acid gurgling in my gut and it's like a gas boiler kicked on, ready to incinerate fat cells and make me stronger. Just like vanquishing that greasy sandwich before it takes up residence in his six-pack abs is Lucas's.

It's what we do and we're not going to stop anytime soon. The grooves in the paths we've dug for ourselves run deep and hard, like tire tracks left by monster trucks in dried mud.

At Lucas' feet, Chester sleeps in a cardboard box, which Lucas liberated from the recycling bin behind the store. He's swaddled in Monika's fuzzy hospital sock, the kind with rubber grips on the soles. I have eight pairs tucked in my bag. They kept giving me new ones even though I refused to wear them. Wearing the grippy socks in lieu of shoes would have been like admitting defeat. Like a declawed cat, resigned to a life indoors.

It paid off, because look at me now? Running. The hospital is 400 miles behind me and the first of five Normals isn't too far ahead.

"Elden said we're about an hour away from the Ohio/Kentucky border."

"Who the hell is Elden?" Lucas asks. He's licking his fingers. God make him stop.

"The guy who cooked you that tasty breakfast sandwich."

"Put it under heat lamps is more like it. And make that two sandwiches and a side of hash browns."

"He let me borrow his phone. I left a voicemail for Monika. She wanted me to let her know I was okay."

He's shaking his head.

"What?"

"You shut me down when I first met you. But you and Elden? Like this." He crosses his index and pointer finger. "You're inscrutable."

"I'm okay with that."

Lucas pulls another wrapped sandwich from his bag. If it were anyone else, I'd worry about food poisoning. But with us two, it's just a matter of who will need a restroom first. I'm about to start the car when Lucas stops me.

"Wait. You're going to need this if you plan on talking to

everyone who gives you coffee," he says, reaching into a corduroy bag and pulling out something furry. I startle, believing for a moment it's another orphaned animal. One is enough. Thankfully Chester sleeps soundly, his chest rising and falling rapidly, paws crossed over his eyes. But when Lucas places the object in my hands I understand.

The wig is the color of desert sand. Golden with cinnamon strata peeking through in equal measure depending on the light.

I run my fingertips along its silky strands, my breath keeping pace with a growing realization. This was no Halloween costume. "This is real hair."

"Yep. Ava, Declan's sister, wore a few different wigs until eventually she was like, screw it, and left her head bare. She owned it. Hair no hair. Either way. She was always pretty. But this one looks most like her."

Declan's sister had cancer. That's what Lucas meant by him having a rough go of it. And Lucas was there for him and so he was there for Lucas, ready and waiting with a getaway car. I close my eyes and let it all sink in.

"You're a good friend, Lucas." Me? I'm always too scared or self-absorbed to be useful to anyone. Thinking about not eating is a real time suck. "I'm sorry about his sister."

Lucas touches my elbow. "Hey, it's okay. She is fine now. In her second year at Temple."

How do I say this without sounding like a total asshole?

"At the hospital, they kept telling me I had a disease. A mental illness. And yet they meted out their cure with such hostility. Treated me like a prisoner. It sucks that Ava had cancer, but there were so many times I wished I did too. Because people rally around cancer and diabetes and heart disease, with 5Ks and lemonade stands. I coveted the sympathy given to other kids at the hospital. The ones with diseases that were more socially palatable."

Lucas doesn't say anything and I assume the worst.

"Something with a possible cure?" he offers. "I get that."

His support makes me more confident. "Yeah. Some disease

I didn't ask for. The doctors, the nurses, the shrinks, they don't say it, but I know what they're thinking. They think I gave this to myself."

I've said too much. Almost broke our most important rule about not talking about food or our respective battles with it.

We lock eyes and it looks like he wants to say something more. But then his face softens, and he puts the baseball cap on.

"Whataya think?" he asks.

I tilt my head then reach over and adjust the brim.

"There. Now, I barely recognize you."

I deadpan then turn away.

"Funny. Try the wig. The other one is pink." He flicks a thumb toward the trunk. "I can get it if you want."

I could never pull off pink. It would attract too much attention. But I ask him to get it anyway. I'm even too self-conscious to try this one on in front of him.

While Lucas is gone, I angle the rearview mirror to see the top of my head and eyes. The shoulder-length wig slips easily over my short nearly black locks and falls snugly into place. Immediately, the color makes my brown eyes browner, and though it's more hair than I've been used to these days, every inch of me feels lighter. Like the heavy Gemma-ness I wear like a chainmail has been lifted and I'm free to be someone new.

Sometimes I get so sick of myself. It's stupid. It's just a wig. But then Lucas pops back into the passenger seat and he sees it too.

"Wow. You look. Wow."

For the first time I'm happy I don't have my phone. There's no temptation to take a selfie. No instant digital image of this moment, one that I can expand with my fingertip until I'm able to peer down my pores like I'm on the edge of a well. Nothing to hold up to all the beautiful girls on IG for comparison. I look good. I see it in Lucas's eyes and more importantly, I see it in my own.

I nod toward the other wig in his hands. "Sorry I made you get that. I think I'm going to stick with this one."

"Your choice. Just like Ava. Wig, no wig. Pink, blond. Doesn't matter. Pretty every way." His matter-of-factness doesn't come off as a come on or crush, but like something he assumes I already know, like he doesn't know his words are like water to a withering cactus.

"Thank you," I say, hoping he can hear the sincerity in my voice.

But he's not paying attention. He's too busy adjusting the pink wig on his head.

He flips one side. "Try not to be jealous."

I laugh. "That is no small task, my friend."

I turn the ignition key and shift the car into drive. It's so quiet, the tires crackle against the loose gravel as I angle the Impala away from the pump and onto the empty, tree-lined road. My skin prickles and heart double pumps at the sight of the endless liminal space before us. I'm torn between wanting to stay here forever and reaching our first Normal.

12

We're at a traffic light about to cross a green steel truss bridge spanning the Ohio River. Mom taught me the names of every type of bridge during our summer road trips. Suspension, beam, arch, tied arch, cable-stayed, cantilever. I know them all. The bodies of water they span. The places they link together.

"That's Kentucky on the other side," I say to Lucas who's been trying unsuccessfully to get Chester to lick some cows milk from his fingertip.

"How did I get stuck with this disgusting job again?"

"No license."

"Riiiight."

The blinker ticks extra loudly, counting the seconds until the light changes and we can cross the bridge to find our first Normal on the other side.

It's weird when you think about it, but bridges solve problems. From a fallen log laying across a stream, to the double-decker George Washington Bridge linking New Jersey with Manhattan. Bridges remove obstacles. Create connections.

Like synapses in our brains.

Lucas groans. "We're not fooling him. He hasn't taken a single drop since our pee break."

As predicted, we made one more stop at a gas station restroom right before the Pennsylvania/Ohio border. I peed a small pot of coffee and Lucas returned from the restroom chewing spearmint gum. No judgement here.

"We need to find a pet store soon," I say.

"Yup. He's cute now, but a hangry raccoon may rip our throats out. Especially when he realizes he's been kidnapped by furless raccoons."

"We didn't kidnap him. We saved him."

"Yeah. I doubt wild animals do nuance. Don't blame me when he goes for your jugular."

Finally, the light changes and I wait my turn in the intersection to make the left onto the bridge. Mid-morning sun sparkles peridot on the rippling water beneath us. I soak in the beauty through triangular snapshot sections, and sense a rush of warmth throughout my body, like the old me is rousing and stretching her bones.

"Make a wish," I say when we reach the bridge's apex, and the tires hum a deep bass note on the steel grating.

"Huh?" Lucas says.

"It's what my mom used to say whenever we crossed a new bridge. Make a wish. Quick before we reach the other side."

"So the wish only works when you're on the bridge?"

"Don't question it. Just do it. Come on, I've already made mine."

Lucas closes his eyes, sending his silent request into the universe with mere seconds to spare before we reach the other side. Ashland, Kentucky. The gateway to Normal.

"Well, Chester is still here so I guess that didn't work," Lucas says.

I ignore him. Some of his jokes are too corny to encourage.

As we drift along the busy thoroughfare, an orphaned raccoon and two damaged beings inside our imperfect vessel, my eyes dart from left to right, hoping we're not attracting any undue attention in our spotted car with out-of-state plates. A familiar fear percolates inside me. Two fears, really. Always at odds. One of being noticed, the other of never being seen.

At the first major intersection, I take in the strip malls, a bowling alley, Starbucks, fast food restaurants, and big box stores of Ashland, all ubiquitous signs of suburbia, but not Normal. Not yet.

I turn left and the Impala glides south along the Ohio River, almost as if it's on autopilot guided by a divining rod following the path toward water.

When we reach the point on Route 23 on the outskirts of

Ashland—the location I circled in my atlas, the place we just traveled more than 400 miles to get to, the place where Normal should be—it's an industrial park with windowless rectangular warehouses. The kind of place you'd hole up to wait out a zombie apocalypse. Rows of cement walls, loading docks, and black-top parking lots. If you closed your eyes and wished to wake up in a place that is the opposite of Paris, this would be it. The vacuous architecture leaves me gutted and so tired. Like, I could pull over to the side of the road and fall asleep right now tired.

At a traffic light, Lucas asks a big question. "This what you expected?"

Valid question given I dragged this kid here. What did I expect from Normal? Up until now, my ideas about a "normal life" have been informed by what I've viewed on a screen. The social media feeds of classmates and influencers, TV commercials for laundry detergent and Cheerios, white picket fences wrapped around craftsman houses, where happy families with the right number of parents and kids in matching pajamas sit around sunlit kitchen tables eating spoonfuls of whole grain goodness, intoxicated by the scent of Ultra Fresh Gain.

To quote Dr. Paige Fucking Bryant, I "deflect."

"Is this what *you* expected?" I ask.

"Me? My expectations couldn't be any lower, which, judging from the current view, is a good thing. I told you. All I wanted was to get away. I didn't care where we were going."

I'm confused. I thought Lucas wanted to reach Normal as much as I did.

"So it was only about the journey for you?"

My disappointment supplanted by indignation.

"Pretty much."

"That's very Ralph Waldo Emerson of you."

"Emerson was a hack. Rumi had him beat by about six hundred years." Lucas quotes, "'As you start to walk on the way, the way appears.'"

"Not quite the same thing."

"I know. It's better."

I frown. "How so?"

"Look, when I first saw you in the common room that day, I only knew two things. I wanted to talk to you and had the overwhelming urge to run. My wrestling season and potential scholarship were quite possibly fucked, and my girlfriend was using me for my jacket and proximity to Declan… Let me put it this way. I'm in Kentucky, holding a baby raccoon, in an old spotted car, with a girl I just met, and you know what? It's better than what's waiting for me at home. I didn't care where I went as long as I got away from where I was."

"Kaitlin is still your girlfriend?" I sound jealous. But of what I can't be 100 percent sure.

"Who knows? So much of who I am, or was, is contingent on me being a wrestler. I really liked her when we started dating, even though I knew I was her second choice."

I reach for him without thinking then second guess myself and touch Chester's tiny, padded paw instead. "I'm sorry."

"S'okay. I'm not completely blameless. I stayed with her for the sex."

Lucas is having sex? I drift into the next lane. A driver lays on his horn. I snatch my hand back and put it on the steering wheel.

My perfect score on the Rice Purity Test almost got us killed. Why should I be shocked? Everyone is having sex, smoking weed, smoking cigarettes, which is far cooler than vaping in my opinion, or drinking vodka stolen from their parents in a park somewhere. Except me.

"The thing about sex is," Lucas continues, "once you start having it, you don't want to stop. Sex complicates things."

Ah. All or nothing brain is something I do have experience with.

"Yes, but if you go long enough without it, your mind will eventually adapt and turn off the sex switch," I offer.

"Really? And you know this because—"

I opt out of revealing my virginity or my ability to turn off my want and need for food.

"To answer your earlier question. I don't know what I was expecting to find in Normal. But figured I'd know it when I saw it. Does that make any sense?" I ask.

Lucas nods. "Kinda, yeah. But whatever that something is would have to be significant. I mean, I've never been tall but if by some miracle, I went from five foot five to six feet overnight, I'd notice."

Would the shift to Normal be that seismic or more subtle like puberty, impossible to see while you're in it but very obvious to someone who hasn't seen you in a while?

"You want to be tall?" I ask Lucas.

"Doesn't every guy? Almost every American president was six foot or better."

"Napoleon was short. Winston Churchill too."

"What's your point?"

"Short people can lead nations."

"A more recent example might have better served your argument."

I shrug. Every girl wants to be thin and beautiful, with plump lips, good skin, and over a million social media followers. She wants to be smart, but not threatening. Pretty, but not in the fake way that makes people not take you seriously. She wants to wake up every day and step out into the world secure in the knowledge that she's good enough. Worthy of having friends and being loved and loving back.

"I have no idea what guys want," I say.

"Trust me. They want to be tall and ripped with good hair and a big—"

"Brain?"

Lucas laughs. "Yeah, sure. And in my case, having all that would make life so much easier."

"Why?"

"Because I could've played football or basketball and wrestled as a heavyweight."

He'd want to be a heavyweight? Hard to imagine. In my world, Skinny wins. Every. Time.

"No woman could ever succeed with the words 'heavy weight' attached to her name," I say.

I sigh as I turn off the main road and attempt to circle back to where we crossed the bridge into Ashland. I'm annoyed that Lucas has yet to acknowledge what I've said, and I'm about to tell him so, when he shouts.

"Look!"

"What the fuck, Lucas? You need to stop scaring me," I say.

"Over there. Ernie's House of Pets."

It's a mostly empty strip mall set way back from the road.

"Weird spot for a pet store. You'd have to know it existed to find it," I say.

"A way appears."

No shit. That Rumi knows what the fuck he's talking about. I hit my blinker and coast onto the shoulder to give myself ample time and space to make a right turn into the parking lot.

"Hanna Gabriels," Lucas says.

"Huh?"

"Women's heavyweight boxing champion. Technically there isn't a heavyweight champ in women's Olympic freestyle wrestling but there is at the collegiate level."

"In other words, you're simultaneously proving me wrong and right?" I ask.

"Just wanted you to know I was listening," he says.

"I appreciate that, but if that's true, then you'd know I was speaking metaphorically," I say while gliding the Impala toward a smooth landing. "It goes beyond sports."

"Noted," he says.

I shouldn't be so hard on Lucas. We both feel the pressure to succeed in the bodies of adolescent boys. For some, being the best isn't enough, we must look a certain way, meet a certain aesthetic, while reaching for a higher bar. Or as Ginger Rogers so aptly described the dance steps she perfected as part of her partnership with Fred Astaire. *Backwards in heels.*

That's exactly how I feel I'm trudging through life sometimes. Backwards in heels.

13

I park the car and fish around for my wallet in my backpack, which is still loaded with books from that last day at school. The day I fainted. It's funny how you never know when you're going to leave a place and never go back. I've got twenty-five dollars in cash and two visa gift cards I got from my paternal grandparents, who retired to Florida five years ago and, except for birthdays and holidays, remain radio silent.

Hopefully, it's enough to buy supplies for Chester. We need to save the cash Lucas got from Declan for gas.

"You go. I'll wait here with Chester," Lucas says.

I look around as I approach the pet store, knowing staying with Chester is not about self-sacrifice, but the opportunity to scarf down another protein bar or else rid himself of more calories. Doubt there's a public restroom nearby. There's nothing else here besides a place called Doors to Go. Would there ever be a time you wouldn't want a door to go? Does one purchase a door and say, *I'll leave it right here on the showroom floor, thanks.*

I must check this out.

I cup my eyes to block the glare and press my forehead to the glass. There are at least five rows of doors extending from the front window to the back of the store, an invitation to the *Twilight Zone.* But instead of Rod Serling, I see a pretty blondish girl with skinny legs peering out at me from the other side of one of the all-glass doors. I jump and so does she. That's when I realize. Duh. It's me. And suddenly Snow White turns into the evil stepmother in the magic mirror.

Stupid door store.

I adjust my wig and open the pet shop door. Inside Ernie's, I'm greeted by a squawking macaw. "Hello! They're stealing the crickets!" it croaks from its perch behind the counter.

The woman behind the counter looks at me and rolls her

eyes. "Ignore the bizarre-o bird. My husband taught him to say that. Says it keeps people on their toes." Her voice warbles as she speaks to me from the other side of an oscillating fan. Is there a band of cricket thieves carousing around Ashland? I want to ask, but don't.

I'm beginning to sweat. Ernie's is greenhouse balmy. Tropical birds need tropical temps. But at the pet store where I worked, there was a separate bird room to avoid window condensation and high heating bills. Apparently this guy, wrapped in royal blue and sunflower yellow plumes, has free reign of the store and crowned himself king.

I laugh. "He's beautiful."

She peers around the fan. "How'd you know he's a he?"

"Good guess. He's big, for one. And his cere is dark blue."

A female's cere, or soft nose above the beak, is lighter-colored and lady birds are generally smaller. The only real way to tell is with a blood test or if the bird lays eggs.

"Good eye," she says.

The small storefront shop is packed floor to ceiling with fish tanks, cages, reptile habitats, and supplies. The place reminds me of Just Pets. Same earthy-smelling mix of dog and cat kibble. Same undercurrent of fish and rodent poop. I inhale. Bliss. I passed my summer days there with the animals, reading a book behind the counter when we were slow, which was most weekday afternoons. No social pressures. No one bugging you to eat lunch and dinner. I worked from one to seven p.m. most days. Perfect hours for passing up Dad's spareribs or Gram's manicotti. She'd started cooking for us after Mom died and years later still showed up at dinner time with enough food for a family of six. I'd tell her I ate at the store.

"Can I help you find something?"

"I hope so. I rescued a baby raccoon."

"From where?"

"The middle of the road." My voice rises into a question.

"What road?"

This unexpected inquisition has me all flustered. "Uh, about two hours away from here. In Ohio." Or maybe it was West Virginia. I'm losing track.

"Did you check around for the mom?"

"Yes. She was dead."

"Other babies?"

"Well, I…I didn't see any. I mean, I looked around but it was dark, and he was in the middle of the road."

The woman, who I assume is Mrs. Ernie, puts up her hand. "Stop right there. Have you ever raised a baby raccoon before?"

"Uh, no."

I'm regretting my honesty.

"Then you're already in over your head. Do yourself a favor and call an animal control officer or wildlife rehabilitation center. It needs to be checked for worms and immunized for rabies, and distemper. Does it have teeth?"

"A few little ones."

"Probably on the verge of being weened. It's going to have to be bottle fed."

"Yes, that's why I'm here. Do you sell kitten formula? He's hungry."

Her hard stare penetrates my soul.

"Come on." She ambles out from behind the counter and I follow her to the back of the store, where the cat food is. "We have a premixed can for ten dollars and the powered kind for $22.50. The can will probably hold you over until you can unload the little bugger. I've got a name I can give you."

My pet store sold the same stuff. Once you open the can, the formula needs to be refrigerated.

"Better give me the powder." It hurts to be paying more than double, but I have no choice and no immediate plans of getting rid of Chester.

She narrows her eyes and takes the powered formula from the shelf. "Suit yourself. You'll be needing an eyedropper or baby bottle. I sell them as a set for $2.99."

Crap. I'm now over twenty-five dollars before tax. "Perfect, thanks."

She walks me down the aisle to the pet meds section and takes the feeding kit off a hook.

"Anything else?"

I'm tempted to get a pet carrier or sling but they're too pricey. Repurposing my backpack for Chester makes more sense. "Blanket?"

"Fleece? $6.99?"

"Sure."

Raising kits is expensive.

At the register, the macaw opens his beak and squawks again, but before he has a chance to accuse me of cricket theft, Mrs. Ernie scolds him. "Shut it, Melvin," she snaps. Surprisingly, Melvin complies.

"Thirty-four dollars and forty-three cents," Mrs. Ernie says after she bags my purchases and scribbles something on the back of my receipt. "That there is the name and address of an experienced animal rescue volunteer. Go see her."

I hand over one gift card and accept my receipt, which shows a balance of $15.57. "I definitely will," I say.

She knows I'm lying.

"Good luck. Here's a piece of advice for what it's worth. Let it go. You can't teach a baby raccoon manners. You'll never be its momma."

Someone should teach Mrs. Ernie and her stupid bird some manners. I suddenly have the urge to steal every fucking cricket in the store.

"See you around, Melvin," I say, then walk out the door.

14

S crew you, Mrs. Ernie," I say as I slip into the driver's seat. "I'll be his momma if I want to be his momma!"
"I take it that didn't go well?" Lucas asks.

"She thinks we should find an animal rescue that will take him."

Lucas doesn't say anything. I give him a hard stare with raised eyebrows that clearly says, *Come on, waiting for you to agree with me here.*

"Want me to tell you all the reasons Mrs. Ernie is right?"

"No."

"Let's start with the obvious. Raccoon."

"Here we go."

"Rabies. Disease. Smelly raccoon shit. Cat killer."

"Will you stop with the cat killing, enough!" I roll down the window. My blood is boiling.

Lucas clearly isn't finished. "Okay, how about someday this cute little raccoon is going to be a big, nocturnal raccoon with opposable thumbs that can, at best, rummage through your drawers while you sleep and, at worst, strangle you."

"I'll worry about that when the time comes."

"When the time comes? Are you seriously considering keeping this thing?" Lucas' cheeks are flushed. The neck crack is coming. Yup. There it is.

I slam the steering wheel with my palm. "Chester. His name is Chester. And apparently you and Mrs. Ernie have no idea how badly I've always wanted a pet. Cat, dog, guinea pigs—growing up I would have taken anything. But my dad didn't want the added responsibility. Munchkin the dwarf frog was about all he could handle," I say in one long burst. "And you said it yourself. Chester is cute."

"I did not!"

"Did too! And a pet raccoon with its little dexterous hands would be adorable, like having a toddler around."

"You say that like it's a good thing."

But what about when you go away to college? I can hear Dad say. *Who will watch it?* That was always his reasoning for why we couldn't have a domesticated fur baby, which let's be honest, would have been a surrogate sibling for me. But I imagine raccoon sitters aren't easy to come by. Fuck it. I'll worry about that next year. I still need to get into college. I still need to apply to college. I also need to figure out how to keep Chester alive until I leave for college and find us a better Normal, and all we have is the sucky burner phone with no internet access. My thoughts are spiraling.

I turn the key in the ignition and put the car in drive. "We've got to find a library," I say.

"Whoa. Let's pace ourselves. We don't want to do all the fun stuff before noon."

My eyes dart sideways to see if he's joking. He is. Lucas is a nice counterbalance to my Camus meets Eeyore world view. *Nobody realizes that some people expend tremendous energy merely to be normal.* Oh, bother.

"Let's head back toward the center of Ashland. That's where libraries usually live. Obviously, I need info on raccoon care and the other Normals. See where we should go next." I also want to check my college board site to make sure my rec letters came in so I can apply early admission to Columbia. But I don't tell Lucas that.

Ten minutes later we find a park in the center of Ashland. Central Park. Like the one in New York City in name only. A block off the park on Central Avenue is the Boyd County Public Library. Bingo.

I navigate the parking lot and slip our giant vehicle into a space. I'm able to pull all the way through to the empty spot facing outwards so I won't have to back up when we leave.

"What about Chester?"

I grab my bag from the backseat and empty out my books.

"I'll put him in here. He'll be fine. I won't be long."

I line the backpack's bottom with his new fleece blanket and settle a sleepy Chester in with his tiny bottle containing powdered kitten formula. I'll get water inside the library.

As we approach the entrance there's a pumpkin-shaped poster on an easel by the front door.

Halloween Pet Parade Today @ 3 pm!
All costumed critters are welcome!

"Shit, if we'd known we could have dressed up Chester like a famous rodent like—"

"Remy?" I offer. I loved *Ratatouille.*

"Nicodemus. That's a name with balls."

"Look at you with the *Mrs. Frisby and the Rats of Nimh* reference."

"What? I loved that book," Lucas says.

"Me too. Rats are rodent geniuses."

A fitting allusion for a pair of escaped lab rats.

I think of the five a.m. wakeups to draw blood, check our temps, weight, and orthostatic blood pressure check. The threats if we didn't finish breakfast in thirty minutes. The sporks as our only utensil with our napkin-less meal because somehow, they thought we'd be able to hide scrambled eggs, bacon, toast, and fruit under a one-ply sheet.

Lab rats get treated more humanely and have certain death to look forward to, I conclude.

Inside the automatic doors the scent of coffee and books greet me.

"Smells like home," I say.

I take in the autumnal-themed display with Halloween picture books and classic horror like *It* and the *Exorcist.* The pre-Halloween-pumpkin-decorating contest in the children's area and the round-faced girl in a ladybug costume, who reminds me of myself when I was five. Back when cherubic cheeks and a squishy belly were cute. Enjoy it while you can, I want to tell her. It won't be long before the wolves turn on you. Second grade by my estimation. That's when I went to my first pool party in a two-piece mermaid bathing suit that made me feel as pretty as Ariel until Hannah Lewandowski told me I looked like a puffer fish, and I spent the rest of the party wrapped in a towel or hiding in the bathroom until my mom picked me up.

A library page in a flowy black witch costume whisks by with a cartload of books while another, dressed like a Minion, helps a patron with the self-checkout machine thereby negating the concept of self-checkout.

These are my people.

Back home, I spent many an afternoon cocooned in a study carrel, among friendly librarians and book nerds who, like me, silently haunted the stacks and got their thrills from free Wi-Fi and coffee vending machines. The next best thing to the pink-nosed guinea pigs and saltwater fish at Just Pets.

But "Familiar" isn't the same as Normal. It's transient. More like a déjà vu, than a place with permanency or potential.

Lucas struts up to the circulation desk while I scan for public computers. There's a row of PCs in front of the reference desk on my right.

"Gonna walk around town. Want anything?" Lucas says when he returns.

I want a lot of things, but Lucas means food.

"No thanks. I'm going to print out some info on baby raccoon care and the other Normals on our list. My outdated road atlas isn't very helpful."

"You think?"

Lucas turns to leave, and I stop him. "Wait—"

"Extra almond milk and stevia. I got you," he says.

I smile as he walks away. I guess he does.

The reference librarian sets me up on a public PC and shows me how and where to print documents. I sign on to my college board account first, the place where my transcript, test scores, and rec letters are kept so I can submit my college applications. Early decision apps for Columbia are due by November 1, about thirty-six hours from now. I worked so hard for this.

Grades were the one thing about high school I could control. All those hours spent alone studying, perfecting term papers and PowerPoints. It can't be for nothing. I'm itching to reread my essay, but I know I'll find something I want to change or improve and there isn't time to dive headfirst down that particular rabbit hole. So I press send. In a month, I'll know if I got into my first choice.

I log out and get started on my raccoon research.

A dozen or so internet searches later and I'm armed with information about raising rescued raccoons—Mrs. Ernie warned me, it's not for the faint of heart—and nearby campsites, which serve the dual purpose of being cheap and good hiding places. I've also found out enough about the other Normals on our list to know there's only one worth visiting. Normal, Illinois. A mere seven hours and 434 miles from here. Wish I knew that before I left the hospital. How did people live without the internet? The accumulating unanswered questions would have consumed me.

I ease open the zipper on my bag to search for a pen and paper to write down a few research details. While feeling around inside the laptop pouch, which protects my atlas from Chester, my fingertips brush against what feels like the rough texture of the oversized notecards I use for studying. I ease it out, careful not to wake Chester who's flat on his back with a paw draped over his eyes, and discover it's not a notecard at all, but a square-ish envelope. I'm about to open it when out of nowhere Chester lets out a soul-piercing cry. My face goes hot as heads turn and all eyes fall on me. Their expressions all say the same thing. *What the?*

"Sorry! Wildlife ringtone! Forgot to silence my phone."

I shove the envelope back in the bag, pinch closed my backpack flap with the other, and dash toward the ladies' room with Chester screeching all the way. *No, no, no, no, no.* This isn't happening. I'm mortified, but it's not his fault, it's mine. He must be starving.

Inside the restroom I fumble getting the top off his bottle

and add water to the powdered formula. "One more minute, little guy, I promise." I shake his bottle then fumble to get some droplets of nourishment down his throat. My soothing reassurances are having absolutely no effect. If anything, he's getting louder, and the bathroom acoustics are making it sound like Chewbacca's in here passing a kidney stone. I need to make a break for it before someone comes to investigate. So, I zip him up and sprint for the exit, fake coughing all the way to mute his cries.

Outside, Lucas runs toward me carrying a to-go coffee cup and white paper bag, stained with grease.

"Ohmygod, you won't believe—" I start.

But Lucas hustles right past me toward the parking lot. "The car. Now!"

I jog after him, trying not to jostle Chester, who's still crying.

"Keys." Lucas dances in place like he needs to pee.

I pull them from my pocket but keep them in a balled fist. "Not until you tell me what's going on."

"Our parents have been in touch. They're looking for us."

This is not completely unexpected. My dad is fiercely protective of me. It was only a matter of time before he connected the dots and sought out Lucas's parents. I take a deep breath.

"How do you know?"

He waves the burner phone. "Dec. My parents called him."

"Did he tell them we're with him?"

"He tried. No one was buying it. He's crashing with a friend at Penn State for the weekend, but I can't ask him to keep lying."

"Of course not."

My teeth hurt and my head buzzes, signs that my hunger is winning this standoff.

"Even if they know where we are, which they don't, we'll be gone before anyone can get to us," I say.

"For now. What if state police issues one of those alerts with our yearbook photos?"

Ugh. My fat photo? The entire state of Pennsylvania would see my fat photo from junior year? The thought makes me dizzy and oh God, what if Jersey's state police get involved and kids at my school find out?

"Fuck," I say.

He'll do it. I know my dad. He'll call out the National Guard if he has to. He always overreacts. I'm sure Gram gave him my message. Why can't he believe I'm okay and give me time? I close one eye. Open it, then close the other. Try not to sway while standing. Chester's still crying, or is that me? The flashing lights in the corner of my eyes make it difficult to focus right before the blackness closes in.

"Gemma? Are you okay?"

White noise engulfs me, a piercing whinny like a power saw. My knee joints come unhinged and my legs fold backward. Gibberish slips from between my lips when I try to speak. I reach for Lucas, even though I no longer see him, then pitch forward toward the pavement.

15

Drink." Lucas holds something to my lips and I obey. Sugary goodness fizzles on my tongue. This isn't my coffee, and it can't be non-caloric. First rule of dieting. If it tastes good, don't eat it. But I swallow automatically, satisfied by how good a *real* Coke, not brown liquid with artificial sweetener, can taste. I take another gulp before I change my mind.

My stomach gurgles a reminder of its emptiness.

"Gatorade would be better for your electrolytes, but this should help your blood sugar levels," Lucas says. "I threw out your coffee. It'll only dehydrate you."

I'm in the front passenger seat of the car with my legs hanging out the open door. There's dirt and gravel on my stinging palms and my right elbow hurts. We're still in the library parking lot and I can't be sure, but I think I smell fries.

Chester!

"Where's my bag?"

Lucas nods toward the passenger side floor. Chester's ensconced in his box. My backpack is beside it. Phew.

"Did I pass out?"

"You scared the shit out of me that's what you did. You pitched forward but I got to you before your head hit the ground."

In all my months of restricting calories, I'd only ever fainted that one time in gym class. Seems like the only kind of attention I garner is the wrong kind.

Lucas is right, I'm probably dehydrated. But also, when I got admitted to the hospital my red blood counts were low, and I had thiamin and potassium deficiencies. All three can cause heart problems. I bitched about the daily poking and prodding at the hospital, but at least I knew what was going on inside my body. What if something's wrong with my heart?

Bad things happen when you don't eat. My fucking therapist's mantra.

Bad things happen and *then* you don't eat, I fired back at her. But she just pursed her lips and stared me down. *Prove me wrong was* her passive-aggressive way of ending our sessions. I plan on surviving if only to do just that.

"I wonder if they know Monika helped us run away," I say. "I'm still not sure why she did."

"Just a guess here, but maybe she liked you?"

We weren't friends in the conventional sense, the normal sense. But the flimsy hospital curtain didn't prevent us from breathing each other's secrets and fears. I owe her a debt which I hope to someday repay.

"Have they announced our names?" I ask.

Lucas shakes his head. "Declan didn't say."

"Do they know about the car?" I ask.

"Not yet. Maybe we should ditch this burner phone and get a new one. Avoid public places. I need a better disguise than a baseball hat and sunglasses."

A man walks by the front of the car with a wiener dog dressed like a burrito. I look at Lucas.

"I'm not dressing up like a burrito," he says.

"Don't be ridiculous. We can't afford a burrito costume. You did look pretty in the pink wig. With some cheap zombie make-up, we'd be unrecognizable."

Lucas doesn't say no. I scoop up Chester.

"I should feed him," I say.

"You should. He *needs* to eat."

His tone and stare are deliberate. My face gets hot.

"What's the point if he spits it up?"

Two can play the passive-aggressive game.

I press Chester against me and try to get him to take more bottle. His back rises and falls, pushing against my palm. He opens his mouth, then recoils. This stuff smells like morning

breath tastes. I don't blame him for not drinking it. Remember-
ing the syringe, I manage to get a few squirts of formula down
his throat before he clenches his jaw shut. He nuzzles my neck
and I brush his nose with my thumb. It's dry and a tad warm.

Mom used to press her lips against my forehead and knew in
an instant if I were feverish. I have no idea what a dry raccoon
nose could mean. Mrs. Ernie was right. I'm not his momma.

"We should get going. Another burner phone and zombie
make-up can wait," Lucas says.

I attempt to stand, but Lucas guides me back down to seated
and motions for me to swing my legs into the car. Dizzy and
nauseous, I close my eyes to let my insides settle. "Don't even
think about it. Buckle up. I'll drive. You navigate," Lucas says.

My brain pulses like it's too big for my skull. I don't have the
energy to argue. Lucas shuts my door and walks around to the
driver's side. I attempt one more dropper full of formula before
returning Chester to his box, to Monika's hospital sock, before
picking up my road atlas.

"Make a right out of the parking lot, then another right at
the stop sign. Head toward Forty-Fourth Street."

I don't tell Lucas, but I need to see what's left of Normal,
Kentucky, before we head out of town. Partly because I don't
know how to stop. I never quit reading a book I don't like or
drop a class that's too hard. A body in motion must stay in
motion. Inertia, however misguided, that's me. But this time,
it's more than my compulsion for perfection and completion. I
have a bone to pick with God.

Lucas hands me the greasy white bag he's been holding. I
peer inside and inhale.

Mmm, fries.

My mouth waters.

I reach into the bag, pull one out, and take a baby bite. Even
cold, it's salty and delicious. One won't kill me. But the fry
grows thick on my tongue. I grab a napkin and spit it out. Tears
press behind my eyes. I crumple the bag shut and slam it on the
seat between us.

Lucas looks stricken.

Even if we don't talk about them, they're always there. The eating disorders we were forced to name. They stretch out in the ample backseat, hands behind their heads, smug expressions on their faces. Other times, they sit between. Both of us are feeling them now, a light breath on our cheeks, along our arms. My skin prickles. *There is no Normal. You're freaks,* they say. *Why not enjoy the ride?*

16

The Normal Presbyterian Church sits on a grassy slope facing the Ohio River, across the street from a lumber yard and pawn shop. I imagine St. Joseph at one and the devil at the other, plying their dueling trades.

Sure Joseph, Jesus's kind stepdad, provides the raw materials to create, but Lucifer is patient. He leans against a glass counter filled with the former possessions of the desperate. Wedding bands and diamond earrings. A pocketknife with an ivory handle. A half-smirk on his face and an unbuttoned silk shirt exposing a much-too-hairy chest, he thrums his fingers and bides his time until the good Christians cross the road to sell him their souls when prayers fail.

Location. Location. Location.

The red brick church has white columns and matching double doors. The single copper spire is turning greenish, a tarnished directional arrow pointing heavenward. It's a simple structure. The kind of church a second grader would draw.

"What are we doing here?" Lucas is impatient.

"Relax. This will only take a minute."

I direct Lucas to a side street, where we park and exit the car. I trudge up a small knoll, Chester in tow with Lucas a few steps behind.

"Normal Presbyterian Church," Lucas reads the sign then sits on the step below me.

"We came all this way. I had to see what was left of Normal. This church and Mordecai's house. He was the founder of the Normal School. That's how the town got its name."

"*Boring* would have been more apropos," Lucas says, shielding his eyes from the midday sun.

"That's in Oregon."

Lucas squints one eye.

"You're an odd girl, Gemma."

"Odd? That the best you got?"

I slip my backpack from my shoulder gently so as not to wake Chester, hold it by the top loop, and walk toward the door with Lucas right behind me.

"We really should get going."

"I'd like to lodge a complaint with God first," I say.

"I don't believe that's how churches work," Lucas says.

"Really? I haven't been inside one since my mother died."

The heavy wooden door makes a sucking noise, like breaking the vacuum seal on an airtight jar. A puff of air smacks me in the face. Burning candles and stagnation—smells about right.

"May I help you?" The voice startles me as soon as we cross the threshold. A woman with an old-fashioned teased-out updo is coming down the stairs to our right. Choir director or ghost? I can't be sure.

"You see her too, right?" I whisper.

Lucas nods. Good. I clear my throat. "Yes, we're here to lodge a comp—"

Lucas steps in front of me

"Pray. We're here to pray," he says.

"Pussy," I whisper.

"Well, we're gettin' ready for a wedding, but I suppose it'll be okay. The florist isn't here yet."

"Thank you," I say.

"Uh-huh. Go right on in when you're ready," she answers, then clacks down the short center aisle in her sensible blue Clarks pumps before disappearing through a door in the sanctuary.

Lucas and I follow her path. When I step from the red-carpeted vestibule and onto the hardwood floor, something dislodges in my heart and torpedoes toward my brain with the same force it took to open the church door. I am nine years old, trailing in my mother's wake, all eyes on me. A white cloth with a gold crucifix embroidered on top, enshrouding my mother's coffin. We're ushered to the front row, Dad, Gram, and me.

Together but alone in our grief. Dad lost his soul mate, Gram lost her daughter, and I lost my everything.

I grab onto the pew's end to steady myself. Muscle memory takes over and I cross myself and genuflect before sitting down near the aisle. I do pray. But not to God. I ask my mom to look out for Monika. *She's afraid to go to Colorado alone,* I tell her.

I shouldn't have dragged her into this.

Forgive us our trespasses as we forgive those who trespass against us.

Then I plead with her to help me be skinny *and* healthy. To calm my insatiable appetites and let me be both. To make eating more like breathing. Natural. Necessary. Guiltfree. But my brain has been hard-wired for destruction, just like Monika's, and I'm not sure Mom or prayers or any amount of therapy can prevent what's going to happen to me any more than Mom could have willed herself to survive an uncurable autoimmune disease. Her body turned on her. My mind betrayed me. *Am I always going to be this way, Mom? Will I ever be normal?*

"Ha!"

Lucas interrupts the conversation in my head, answering the question he didn't know I asked.

"I think church lady is spying on us through the crack in the door. Probably thinks we're going to steal the hymnals and raid the poor box," he says.

"There's nothing to see here."

"Except, perhaps, the baby raccoon in your backpack."

"God loves all creatures great and small." I unzip the top to check on our *extra* small creature. Poor guy. He's hidden by my atlas and the envelope I was going to use as scrap paper back at the library, before I got all frazzled. I pull out both now to put them in the pocket where they belong. When I do, the envelope flutters to the floor and a photo falls out. Lucas picks it up before I can get to it. I grab the envelope.

"Is this you?"

I take the photo from him. It's a girl about my age, in shorts and a tank top with big hair, even bigger boobs than I used to have, and a smile that lights up her pretty cherubic face. Tanned, curvy, gorgeous. She's leaning against a fence. Sand and ocean stretch out behind her. It could be any beach, any town, but I know exactly where she is.

It's funny how the mind can see beyond the edges of a photograph.

There's a Ferris wheel to the left, which towers over the carousel and kiddie coaster, the "fishies" we called it, with cars painted to look like Dory, Marlin, and Nemo. It was my favorite. To the right is the place with the best soft serve ice cream and waffle cones on the boardwalk. In the foreground, standing in front of the stand with the giant lemon on top, is my dad. He's taking a picture of his future wife, the most beautiful woman either of us had ever seen.

"It's my mom," I say. "This was her prom weekend."

I've heard the stories a million times. Four couples crammed into a motel room meant for two. The owner who kicked them out a day early, forcing them to sleep in their cars. I wish I could hear Mom tell it once more.

"You look just like her, except—"

I push away the compliment. Challenge Lucas with my eyes.

"Except she didn't have anorexia?"

Lucas hands me the photo.

"Except for the smile," he says.

I slip the photo back into the envelope. My mom and dad had dated since they were fifteen. Navigating high school would have been so much easier with a hand to hold, with someone who thought I was beautiful.

"Do you always carry that around with you?"

"No. It's usually tucked into the mirror on my dad's dresser. The envelope fell out of my atlas when I was at the library. I didn't have a chance to look at it before Chester started yowling."

"Yowls? There's something worse than the crying."

"It's more like a weird chittering actual—" I trail off. Why did Dad wait to give it to me? Actually, he didn't even give it to me. He gave me the atlas but never mentioned the precious pearl inside. Was he just hoping I'd find it? What if I hadn't? It could have dropped onto the library floor and been lost forever. And yet somehow, against all odds, my mother found me in a Presbyterian church in Kentucky.

Mom. One name. Three letters. Like God.

I think of all the women known by a single name. Because they're badass and arrived on this planet to change it or save it with music, words, art, acting, news reporting. And you know what everyone cares about more than what they've given us? How much they weigh. We reduce a woman's worth to the size of her jeans or the number on the scale. I used to be disappointed when one of them would cave and crash diet or get surgery, but now I get it. How else will they ever be taken as seriously as men?

We have been sizing up women for thousands of years. I'm going to live and die never knowing what it would feel like to not have that kind of pressure. I could cure everything from premature balding to early-onset Alzheimer's, and the only thing people would be talking about at the press conference is what I was wearing and what I looked like.

Mother is the name of God on the lips of children. I've seen that in memes and tattoos on Pinterest. I don't know if I got it exactly right, or who said it. But what I do know is that God, the real one, was a mother, not a father.

17

After my mom died, I didn't go to school for three weeks. At first, I didn't want to. Then, I didn't know how to.

Mom had always dropped me off and picked me up. She was a part-time classroom aide two towns over, and though we lived within walking distance to Spring Garden Elementary School, she wanted to see me walk into the building.

"I know it's silly, but I need to know you got there safely," she always said.

I never complained, but secretly I hated being treated like a baby and looked forward to sixth grade when I could take the bus to middle school. After she was gone, those thoughts haunted me. I begged God for a do-over. If He brought Mom back, I promised I wouldn't complain. Even if she drove me to school every day until I graduated high school. Either He didn't get the message or chose not to waste a miracle on me.

That first day back on my own was a disaster. Fourth graders aren't well-versed in social niceties as it is, and Girl with Dead Mother Returns was way beyond their capabilities. Mine too.

They acted like death was contagious and I was the cootie kid.

In the cafeteria, my presence silenced the light-hearted chatter of the girls I usually ate with. They came to a hard stop five feet before our table when they saw me, then motioned to each other with their eyes to sit elsewhere. I pretended to tie the laces on my black Converse so I could swipe away my tears. But one boy, Gus Manetti, a fifth grader who lived down the block from me, saw what happened and came over to sit with me. Our moms had been friends and Mrs. Manetti was my emergency contact in town. I still know her number by heart.

"So, do you think the groundhog is going to see his shadow

tomorrow or what?" he had said as he threw one leg over the attached bench. "My guess is six more weeks of winter."

I remember, so clearly—the lung-crushing vice around my ribs released and I could finally breathe. Once he sat down, his friends followed. Like circling wagons, they shielded me from being the cheese standing alone in the middle of the cafeteria. Not just that day, but each day until the girls eventually drifted back, more because of the boys than my subsiding raw emotions, I'm sure. I don't know how he knew, but Gus said and did the exact right thing. It's no wonder I developed an immediate crush on him, one that lasted until he graduated last year.

He never seemed to notice.

What if Lucas is like Gus? One more person who means more to me than I do him. I have no way of knowing. But something flickered in me the night I left the hospital. A lone firefly on a starless night.

The problem is, there will be no one like Lucas or Gus waiting for me at school and I've been gone even longer than when my mother died. What will people say about me this time?

I hold Mom's photo against my chest and stare out the window while Lucas drives the Impala. After taking two more dropperfuls of formula, Chester fell asleep in his box. The tires hum on the smooth road and the wind sounds like the flap of a canvas sail as it pours through the driver's side window, which Lucas has cracked open. We say nothing, but I sense Lucas throwing worried glances my way every few seconds.

"My mom had a rare autoimmune disease," I say, saving him from the curiosity that's nearly killing him. "Scleroderma. Like one in a billion people get it. Even less people die from it. Lottery odds. Lucky her."

"What was she like?"

No one ever asks me that. It's always the obligatory "I'm sorrys" or hollow platitudes like "She's always with you." Blah blah. But his rare question is gift. It churns up all these crystal-line memories, depositing them into my lap, like rough ocean waves planting sea glass on the sand. I rush to gather up these found gems before they're swept out to sea again.

"Her name was Josephine, but everyone called her Josie, or Jo."

"Wise choice."

"Agreed. People said I was her mini me."

Lucas nods. "As is evidenced from the picture."

I want to tell him that I often wonder if that makes it harder for my dad. But it's too icky and Freudian to share, and so I keep talking about Mom instead.

The memories come one after another in no particular order, and with little effort on my part, like scrolling through my newsfeed with my thumb. Lucas is patient as I tell how birthdays and holidays were all Mom, the way she left me notes from the Tooth Fairy written on tiny pieces of paper in microscopic handwriting, the Canadian road trip and my utter surprise at hearing her speak French, how she slept on my bedroom floor whenever I got sick with a fever, and how she tried so hard to teach me about football so I'd watch college games with her on Saturdays.

"She made ordinary things into events. She was fun. And funny."

"I guess the similarities end with your appearance."

I ball a fist and Lucas throws up an elbow to block me, laughing.

"Yeah. But honestly the best part about my mom was that she was always there for me. Until she wasn't."

Lucas puts his hand on the seat between us, palm up. I reach for him without hesitation, and he gives my hand a double squeeze—*you all right?* I squeeze back once—*yes*. We stay that way for the next hour, neither of us letting go until we reach our next stop. I forgot how much I miss having a hand to hold.

"I don't know what you plan on being when you grow up, but you can take Girl Scout Troop Leader off the list," Lucas teases me.

"And you can take stand-up comic off yours. I never said I knew how to assemble a tent."

We're at a campsite in Daniel Boone National Forest about one hundred miles west of Ashland. Evening sun cuts through the nearly leafless oaks and copse of trees beside the lake where we're attempting to set up camp. We chose this sight for its privacy, though it being this late in the season, the campsite is quiet.

Lucas groans. "What the actual fuck?"

Was quiet.

With the exception of the two poles Lucas holds in his hands, our tent lies in pieces on the gravel beneath our feet. Never having been camping before in my life pretty much renders me useless. Plus, I'm so tired my teeth and eyeballs hurt.

"Remind me why I signed up for this again?" Lucas says.

"It was your idea, remember? You were all like 'I can get us a car.' Remember that?"

"Yeah, well. That was before wildlife rescue got added to the bingo card."

"What's that supposed to mean?"

"The raccoon was not part of the plan!" Lucas cracks his neck. His cheeks are flushed and he won't look at me.

Chester is coiled up in the hood of a sweatshirt I've tied around my waist like a makeshift BabyBjörn. Sleep calls out to me from the Impala's backseat, as the shadows grow long and Lucas's patience short.

"I'm done," I say.

"Come on. One more try. We can do this."

I shake my head and begin walking away.

We've been up for seventeen hours and the sun will be setting soon.

"I need sleep. I'm going to lie down in the car."

Lucas is still slamming tent parts around when I reach the car, roll down each of the Impala's four windows halfway, and settle into the backseat. A crisp breeze sweeps across the water, carrying the promise of long, cold November nights. Hard to believe tomorrow is the last day of October.

Chester curls up beside me in his box on the floor. He's so lethargic and his nose has gone from dry to crusty. I'm worried. When we got here, I was able to get a few more syringefuls of formula into him, but he spit it up. He's not eating enough, but maybe it's because he doesn't need milk anymore. At eight weeks baby raccoons can begin eating solid food. I have no idea how old he is.

My head on a balled-up sweatshirt, I close my eyes with Mom's photo rising and falling on my chest—a featherlight passenger made heavy.

I awake in darkness with Chester sleeping on my growling stomach. The thought of him climbing all that way buoys me.

"How did you get up here by yourself, little man?" He looks so cozy I could squeeze him.

Deep heavy breaths drift from the front seat. After checking to make sure a bear hasn't crawled through the open window (it's Lucas) I place Mom's photo back in my bag, mix some formula for Chester, and contemplate what's next while he slowly swallows each five dropperfuls. The relief and happiness that wash over me as he eats makes me think of Dad and turning back. Normal, Illinois, is still more than seven hours away. Factoring in the need to take back roads to avoid being spotted—two kids traveling alone with Pennsylvania plates—it could take us two or even three hours longer. Still, if we leave at midnight, we'd be there by morning.

Chester takes seven whole droppers, which gives him a burst of energy. He explores the backseat, walking up and down my torso, and peering over the edge before settling onto my shoulder with his head under my wig. The rising moon is low and bright.

"Do you know there's a place called Santa Claus in Indiana?"

Lucas calls over the front seat like we've been talking this entire time.

He startled me but I play it cool. "Really?"

"Yup. Right here in your atlas." His hands, and a map of Indiana, rise above the seat.

"I believe you."

"I think we should go."

"Right now? We just got here."

"No. I mean I think we should go to Santa Claus, Indiana. It sounds fun."

"You can't tell very much from looking at a map. Trust me."

"But tomorrow is Halloween. How many times in your life will you be able to say you spent Halloween in Santa Claus? Holidays collide. It's probably mind-blowing. Plus, according to the map it's right next to Holiday World and the Lincoln Boyhood National Memorial."

"Oh well, that changes everything."

He pops his head over the front seat.

"So, you're down?"

No! My pulse quickens. We had a plan. I do not deviate from plans. But for Lucas—

"Thinking about it."

"Fine." He rubs his cheek. "The seatbelt left a weird impression on my face. I need to spread out. I'm going to build a fire and give the tent another shot."

Lucas opens the passenger door. Before he slams it shut, I call after him.

"Hey, why didn't Declan show you how to put the tent together?"

He looks back over the seat again.

"Because he thought he'd be here." That's what Declan meant about me ruining his weekend.

He shuts the car door and lets *that* sink in for a minute.

18

When I emerge from the backseat, I'm struck by the darkness surrounding us and the brightness of the stars. From a hill near my house, on clear nights I can see New York City, the Freedom Tower, the Empire State Building, the yellow halo over the skyline, but stars? Not so much and never this clearly.

Lucas sits beside the fire pit on a rolled-up sleeping bag.

"Hey!" he says.

The flames cast a ruddy glow on his face, making him appear older, his cheekbones more pronounced.

"Hey!" I say back. I sound overly cheerful because I'm worried he's not. "Tent looks good."

The domed lime-green and gray-colored tent sits like a large tortoise near the tree line. It's much smaller than I imagined.

"Wasn't that hard once I put my mind to it."

The temperature has dropped considerably. I'm happy for the warmth of Declan's gloves. He's a conceited jerk, but I'd be lying if I said wearing them didn't give me a tiny thrill. This must be why Lucas's girlfriend won't give up his wrestling jacket.

"Thought maybe you fell back to sleep."

Lucas scooches over and pats the patch of sleeping bag beside him. When I settle in, he hands me a marshmallow on a stick before making another for himself. His kindness melts me, dissolving barriers to emotions I didn't know I had.

"Where's the fur ball?" he asks.

I point to the lump in my jacket and Lucas shakes his head.

"Lucky raccoon."

I'm hyperaware that our side butt cheeks are touching and try, instead, to focus on my marshmallow and the flames.

"Thank you," I say.

"It's just a marshmallow. There's a whole other bag in the trunk."

"Um, the 'thank you' isn't just for the marshmallow. It's for everything."

Lucas waves me off. "Dec hooked us up with all the gear and the snacks."

"He hooked *you* up with gear and snacks for a camping trip, with him. And you shared it with me."

Lucas bumps shoulders with me. "Yeah, but he gave you those stylish gloves."

His words are more sharp than playful, and I regret not leaving them in the car.

"You didn't need me, my license, or my outdated map. You had a plan to escape the hospital all along."

"Kind of. Dec and I were all set to go camping. The plan shifted when I ended up in the ER. As soon as I felt well enough, I told him he needed to help me break out."

"So why didn't you two just go?"

The wood crackles and a few embers fly off the fire. Lucas snuffs them with his foot. Then he strokes his chin, pretending to think.

"Let's see, why didn't I just escape the hospital and go camping with Dec. Oh yeah, I remember. I walked into the common room at the hospital and heard this girl sniping at some dude for mispronouncing her name—"

I jump in.

"And she won you over with her warm, welcoming personality?"

Lucas laughs and his leg falls toward mine. I don't move away. My blood pulses faster, warming me from the inside out.

"Actually, it was the snarky T-shirt. I love a challenge."

This time I bump his shoulder.

"No, seriously, Lucas. I'm such an absolute pain in the ass. You've done all this for me and the only thing I did was mess up your plans with Dec."

"Dec and I can camp whenever. But when will I ever get the

chance to visit Normal, Kentucky, the mysterious gem of the south?"

"Come on, really. Why me?"

My marshmallow catches fire and Lucas takes the stick from me and blows out the flames. I wrinkle my nose when he peels off the bubbly black char.

"Yuck."

"Are you kidding? Burnt marshmallow is the best. Here."

Before I have time to calculate calories or resist, he holds the flambé confection to my lips and I take a gooey bite. It tastes like fire with sugar on top. He's right. It's delicious. And sticky.

"Good, right? Bet you didn't know what you've been missing," he says.

I didn't. Now that I do, I'm not sure I'll be able to give it up.

"I'm adding this to my list," I say.

"What list?"

"My death bed food list."

"Right. This is me pretending I'm not at all alarmed that you have a death bed food list."

Chester adjusts himself and I use it as an excuse to put space between me and Lucas.

"Forget it."

"Forget it? I want to know what else is on it."

I take a deep breath and look him right in the eyes. Okay fine. Let's do this.

"Black raspberry ice cream. An entire tub of pink frosting. Cookie dough. Pizza. Jelly donuts. Fully loaded nachos. A bacon cheeseburger. Empanadas. Peanut butter. Homemade chocolate chip cookies. Eggplant parm and baked ziti. Oh, and grilled cheese."

My mouth is watering.

"You forgot Buffalo wings. Cheesesteak. Funnel cake. Nutella. I'd eat my shoe if it were drizzled in Nutella."

Laughing, I cover his mouth with my hand. "Oh my god, stop." We're breaking our own rules.

When he touches my hand to pull I away, his expression

changes. Something between serious and scared. Shit. I said too much and now he thinks, knows, I'm a freak. But then he lists closer, an almost imperceptible amount, and a warmth spreads over my chest and torso, oh no.

"Lucas?"

"Hmm."

"Chester just peed on me."

"Yeah. That was not on my road trip bingo card either."

19

Chester's chocolate eyes cross as I bring the formula-filled syringe to his mouth. "What happened back there, little man?" I baby talk as I feed him in the Impala's backseat, and I believe Chester knows I'm not only talking about the pee. Nonplussed, he clutches my pinky with tiny fingers while he drinks. I melt. It's impossible to be angry at this much adorableness. It's not Chester's fault nature called when…when what exactly?

I bop him on his nose with my pointer finger. He's too hungry to notice.

My own stomach growls, its juices reignited by burnt marshmallow. It wants more. Denying myself food is getting harder and harder. This is why I'd rather have nothing than be teased with sweetness.

After getting drenched, I wrangled out of my wet fleece, shirt, and bra, in the backseat—using girls' locker-room technique—and slipped on a tank top and tee. Lucas insisted on giving me the Dillsburg wrestling sweatshirt he pilfered from his high school's lost and found. Nick's loss was Lucas's gain. Mine too, I suppose. I didn't want to take it, but Lucas insisted. He had the sleeping bag if he got cold, he said.

Lucas's sweatshirt smells like the fire and him, and it's strange how the latter is so specific and familiar. I smell like, I don't know, a zoo? We need to find a laundromat or more importantly, a place to shower. I don't have a clean bra, and wiping myself down with Wet Ones didn't compensate for Chester's golden shower.

I bend my head so we're nose to nose. He yawns and closes his eyes. "What are we going to do with you, mister? Huh?" After settling him into his box, I stuff my wet clothes into the pet store bag and tuck it under the front seat.

Mom's photo calls to me with all the substance and heaviness of another living thing. I slip it from my bag, stare for a while at my full-cheeked doppelgänger, then close my eyes, willing the universe to let her speak to me once more and growing angrier when I hear only dying crickets and Chester's breathing.

"You have no idea how hard it's been without you."

I'm supposed to be too many things. The girl who eats All the Food and never gains weight, whose virginal body simultaneously oozes innocence and sex. The one who puts herself out there every day on social media, a pouty-lipped, cleavage-popping, creamy-skinned genius with more followers than the social influencer du jour.

I need someone here to tell me I'm perfect the way I am. Even if she's a super-biased mom, I don't care. I'll take it. Though I can't help wondering if I'm ignoring the exact same message from my super-biased dad. Isn't that what he was trying to say with the photo?

The moon is high and the fire smoldering when I step outside with Chester, in a box this time, swaddled in one of my clean socks. A warm amber light glows from inside the tent, framing Lucas's shadow as he alternates between sitting up and laying down. Crunches. I heard him open the trunk a few times and know he's working off whatever he ate while I was changing. I make my footfalls extra heavy, respecting the secrets people like us keep.

Lucas's face appears in the crescent screen atop the zippered "door."

"Don't tell me the flea bag is sleeping with us," he says.

Lucas unzips the flap and holds it open.

"I can't leave him alone. What if he gets hungry or scared?"

"His breath smells like stinky cheese. Keep him on your side of the tent."

I duck my head and scooch inside, where two sleeping bags are cocooned together, like pods.

"There is no my side of the tent."

"By your feet then."

How am I going to do this? I've never slept this close to anybody before.

I start to retreat. "Maybe—"

"What?" Lucas asks.

I was going to suggest I sleep in the car, but I realize, I don't want to be alone.

"I've never slept in a tent before."

"I gathered that when you said you'd never been camping."

I arrange Chester's box at the bottom of my sleeping bag, then crawl to the top. Lucas unzips his sleeping bag and swaddles himself so tightly that only his eyes and nose peek out.

"It's going to be difficult, I know, but try to keep your hands off me."

His joke breaks the tension and I'm able to hunker down in my sleeping bag.

"I'll try to restrain myself," I tease back.

I flip up the hood on Lucas's loaner sweatshirt as an added barrier between me and things that crawl, slither, or jump in the night and roll onto my side. I try not to think about how these flimsy walls won't stave off an attack from a bear or worse, some psychopath with an ax or gun who kills us, burns our bodies, and makes off with the car and what's left of our money.

Camping is fun.

It's so quiet, I can hear Lucas breathing. We're so close, I can *feel* him breathing. His chest rising and falling in the rhythm that lulls a body to sleep. I want to close my eyes but can't. Mom is more alive and present in my thoughts than she has been in years, awakened like a language I knew a long time ago but had forgotten without someone to speak it to. The problem is, the words are spilling over and I have no way of answering her back and so I vacillate between deification and demonization, unsure of how I'm *now* supposed to think of my dead mother.

"Lucas?"

"Huh?" His voice drips with drowsiness.

"Never mind."

I'm not sure what I want to say.

He shifts, and I sense him sitting up. I turn over, and am greeted by his muscular, hairless chest.

"Oh my God, are you naked?"

"What? No!" Lucas flips open his sleeping bag and I shield my eyes.

"Got my boxers on," he says.

I hear the elastic snap and lower my hands.

"You're going to freeze."

"Au contraire, mon frere. It's warmer to sleep with as little clothing as possible."

I twist my mouth. "That makes absolutely no sense."

He puts up one hand. "Swear. Learned it in Boy Scouts."

"So let me understand this. You made it to the meeting when they discussed naked sleeping, but missed the lesson about pitching a tent."

Lucas mock giggles. "You said pitching a tent."

"What are you, seven?" Forgetting his almost full-frontal nudity, I give his chest a shove and the unexpected sensation of my fingertips against his bare skin makes me blush. He grabs my hand before I can pull it back.

"What did you want to say?" he asks.

This was a bad idea.

"It's okay. Sorry I woke you."

He'll wind up meaning too much to me. One way or another, this road trip will end, and he'll go back to Dillsburg and I'll head home to New Jersey, and eventually college. I retract my hand and roll over, pulling my sleeping bag up to my neck. Intimacy on any level is difficult for me, and right now, sharing complicated emotions about Mom is terrifying.

"Gemma." He tugs gently on my sleeping bag. "Come on, talk to me. Are you okay…is this about us breaking Rule Number One?"

Maybe my thoughts about Mom are intertwined with food, but if so, the strands are so knotted and congealed it'd be impossible to tease where one ends and another begins.

I flip back over to face him. "It's the photo," I say. "It's not enough. I always feel so empty."

Lucas lifts his arm for a side hug then, and I lean in without allowing my full weight to press against him, and his half na-kedness. But Lucas pulls me closer, and I allow my shoulders to relax, for my cheek to press against his chest. When he rests his chin on my head, my bones melt away, leaving me soft, without all my sharp edges and no choice but to give in to this comfort. He's a good hugger. A good person. At least with Lucas, talking about Mom is less like picking my way through the thorny bramble of memory, and more like being wrapped in an old, worn quilt.

Eventually he falls asleep, and I slip out from under him and scooch down into my sleeping bag, which has already gone cold. Without fully waking, he rouses and does the same. I'm al-ready lamenting the loss of his touch when he turns on his side toward me and reaches out for my hand. Our fingers interlock on the first try and I don't pull away.

20

The campfire's faint crackle and smoky sweetness nudge my senses awake, like the first pot of coffee on Sunday mornings at home. I reach for both Lucas and Chester, discover them gone and panic. I hate being the last one up. Even in the hospital, the nurses never caught me sleeping. My internal body clock would rouse me before the shift change, giving me ample time to pull myself together so as not to turn anyone to stone with my bedhead or revolting blemishes.

Quick-like, I pull on my boots and flatten my hair and slip on the wig. I forage through my bag for face powder, lamenting the fact that it's the loose kind that does not have a compact mirror, and smack my lips with Blistex before giving my cheeks, chin, and nose a light dusting of "true porcelain." Yeah right. What I wouldn't give to be one of those girls who wakes up looking exactly the way she did when she went to bed. But my subconscious is a scary place and deep sleep wrecks me, leaving me with pillow-marked cheeks and puffy eyes.

Outside, Lucas paces along the tree line, burner phone pressed against his ear, Chester in the crook of his arm. His face is tight and serious, and I wonder who he's talking to and what's wrong. Why else would he risk using the phone?

But the smile he flashes when he sees me is reassuring. I inhale, yogi style, filling my senses with cold, pine, and falling leaves. Slowly, I exhale, bringing my breath and heart back into sync. It wasn't some impending calamity that threatened to send me reeling. It's that I don't want to feel things he doesn't.

"There's instant coffee in the cups and hot water on the fire. Be right there," he calls, then returns to his conversation.

There is indeed a bubbling tea kettle on the grate spanning the fire pit. Beside the stainless-steel coffee cups are two more cups with instant oatmeal. If he's using some kind of loosy-goosy psychology on me it's working. I'm hungry.

I test the tea pot handle to make sure it's cool, then pour hissing water into all four cups and stir. There's even powdered creamer. It's got nothing on almond milk, but I'll take it.

While my coffee cools and the oatmeal thickens, I sit on the log beside the fire and stretch my legs in front of me, deliberately keeping my ankles off the ground so my thighs are suspended and not flayed out like ham hocks.

When Lucas sits down beside me, he lets Chester crawl from his hand onto my lap, then nudges me with his shoulder. *No weirdness between us, right?*

I nudge him back. *No weirdness.*

"That was Kaitlin."

Weirdness. Though I appreciate his honesty, the image of a girl who feeds all my insecurities materializes before me. Diminutive with peachy smooth skin, plump lips, and thighs that have about as much chance of meeting as her ears. I don't even know who she is and already I've determined she's better than me.

"A little early, no?"

"We're used to picking up for each other at all hours."

Something green and bile-like rises inside me. The intimacy I covet, which Lucas shares with Kaitlin and seems to come so naturally for others, eludes me. I have no problem understanding AP physics, calculus, and chem, but without a formula or theory to master, I have no idea how to make friends. Romantic or otherwise. It's the same with places too. If I've been there, I'll never forget them, but there's so many places I've never been by myself.

"How did you meet?" Clearly, I'm a masochist.

"It was right after I got called up to the varsity wrestling team last year. The lightweight tore his ACL and I became the only freshman on the team. I guess she saw one of my matches. Dec told me she was into me. We started talking and just like that, I went from being the smallest kid in his grade, with acne that made my back look like the surface of Mars, to a varsity wrestler with a girlfriend who made other guys jealous."

His voice fills with nostalgic longing, and I grow restless. He'd tried to play it like he was using her for sex after he'd realized he was second choice to Declan, but I can tell now that was just bravado.

"Did you love her?"

Why don't I just stick my hand in the fire?

"I thought I did. Maybe? At best it was a skinny love."

That word. It's Pavlovian. I sit taller and suck in my stomach.

"As in, you loved her because she was skinny?"

"As in, it was a love with no substance. Like the song."

I make a mental note to google the lyrics as soon as I'm able. Lucas goes on.

"Anyway, like I said before, sex complicated things."

Oh lord. My self-loathing kicks up a notch. Lucas has been having sex with a future Victoria's Secret model since the tender age of fourteen and I've yet to kiss a boy. I mean, really kiss a boy.

"You know what I mean, right?" Lucas looks me in the eye, and I turn away.

"No. Actually. I don't. Most days I can't stand looking at myself in the mirror. The thought of someone seeing me naked—" I laugh.

Lucas raises his hand like he's bidding in an auction. "Are you looking for volunteers because—"

I butt nudge him so hard he almost falls off the log. "Lucas, I'm serious."

"So am I! Do you ever give yourself a break?" Lucas is annoyed.

I shake my head.

A guttural groan escapes Lucas's throat. Chester crawls from the crook of my neck, where he's been sleeping, into my hood—or the hood of Lucas's pilfered sweatshirt—and hunkers down.

"Quick question here. Do you think I make a habit of asking

any girl I've only just met to run away with me?"

"Well, now that you mention it. Why did you? You never did answer me."

My gaze hardens and he shoots me a look that makes me believe he now wishes he hadn't.

"Because I saw you sitting there, lost in your own world as you looked at that map, which we now know is horribly outdated. You were so serious but sad too, and I wanted to talk to you. I wanted to make you laugh."

"So you felt sorry for me?"

"Jesus Christ, Gemma. I was drawn to you. Like, I knew you were my people. We belonged in the same box of crayons or whatever."

"Peas in a pod?" I offer.

"Sure, peas in a pod."

He's exasperated. I exasperate people. And people confound me. Especially the ones who are my age. I read their cues all wrong.

"And yet here you were talking to your girlfriend."

"Ex-girlfriend. That's why I called her. We were ending things before I went into the hospital. I wanted to confirm our breakup before—" He closes his eyes and massages one temple, then stands up. I reach for his hand to catch him before he can walk away, but he pulls his fingertips out of reach and so I scramble to my feet to block his path.

"Before what? What were you going to say?"

His shoulders relax in defeat. "Before something happened. I was going to say before something happened."

I search his eyes, worried. "What? What would happen?"

"Gemma. You are the dumbest genius I've ever met."

I'm not dumb. I'm afraid. Afraid of making mistakes. Afraid of being imperfect. Of making a wrong move and leaving myself open to being mortally wounded.

Before I change my mind, I lean in toward Lucas until our lips touch. The kiss is sweet, real, and scares me to death because a taste is not enough. I'm going to want more. The burner phone vibrates in Lucas's pocket between us, and we separate.

"Sorry, I should—"

"Yeah, of course," I say.

Might be his ex wanting him back. He looks at the screen before answering.

"Declan. Hey, bro. What's up?"

I can make out Declan's warm, bass voice, but not his words. Lucas furrows his brow and looks at me.

"He wants to know what we were doing at the Boyd County Public Library?"

"Fuck. Put out the fire, we've got to go," I say.

21

"It was my dad, right? It had to be my dad," I say to Lucas after we've doused the fire and packed up the car.

My dad could find me anywhere. When I was five, I got lost at a water park. By the time I heard my name announced over the PA, he'd already had security shut down every park attraction and close all exits and entrances.

I explain this to Lucas.

"He's the kind of guy who always knows a guy who can get the job done," I say.

Being the best mechanic in town helps. Everyone loves him and there's no shortage of people who'd be willing to do him a favor.

"But you must have left breadcrumbs to follow," he says. "What did you do at the library?"

I think. I wasn't there that long before Chester made a scene. I researched raccoons, Normals, nothing personal that would give away my location except.

"Crap."

"What?" Lucas asks.

We're stopped at a traffic light and I look over at him.

"If you sign on to a private website, like social media or maybe a college admissions account—"

"Can someone trace the IP address?" Lucas is nodding. "Absolutely."

My cheeks burn. He'll think I'm an idiot. The light turns green, and I continue driving.

"I signed on to my Columbia account to apply early decision. The ED deadline's tomorrow," I explain.

Lucas thinks before he answers. "It's possible someone traced the IP address of your log in. But your dad must know some people who know some *people* in order to get that done over the weekend."

"Like every cop in town? I'm so sorry," I say.

Lucas shrugs. "It's done. Nothing we can do except hope Declan's not forced to tell him we're driving this car. And keep going. Unless you don't want to."

"Why would I not want to? Bring on the next Normal."

Lucas cracks open the atlas and we both fall silent as I watch the yellow dotted line in the road slip under the car and wait for Lucas to guide me along the interstate. He's being weirdly silent, and I'm lost in thought, thinking about how this partially blind bobsled driver steered better before he had his vision corrected to 20/20. Turns out seeing, or sensing the icy track without looking too closely was better. He had to scuff up his goggles during the Olympics to make his sightline less perfect. It makes more sense to me now. The idea of seeing without looking and taking the road one small piece at a time.

Finally, Lucas looks up from the map and speaks. "Hey, can I ask you something?"

I hope this isn't about the detour to Santa Claus, Indiana.

"Sure."

"What happened back there? Between us? You're not going to friend zone me, right?" Lucas asks.

I dig my thumbnails into the leather steering wheel, hold on tighter, and steady my breath.

"You wouldn't say it that way if you knew how much having you as a friend means to me."

His expression goes dark.

"Why don't you tell me then."

"Everything. It's everything to me. I've never had a friend like you, Lucas. You're smart, and funny, and loyal, and kind—"

My voice breaks. I'm saying this wrong.

"Incredibly hot. Let's not forget that," he says.

Lucas always knows how and when to make me laugh.

Until now, I've been the human version of those Russian stacking dolls, with the real me buried seven layers deep. This openness I have with Lucas, these moments of being real and honest with someone, are so new and fragile to me, like hummingbird eggs inside a thimble, they fill my heart with the promise that someday they'll take flight. I'm afraid any slight move in the wrong direction will ruin that.

I want him to know how I feel.

"Being with you these past two days. It's the most fun I've had in, like, forever. I don't want this to end when this trip is over and I go back to New Jersey. It can't. Now that I know you, I want to always know you. I want us to talk or message every day. Watch movies together while Face Timing. Know that I can call you any time of the day or night and you'll always pick up. I don't need a boyfriend. I need a—"

"Ride or die?" Lucas offers.

"Sure, yeah. A ride or die."

"It doesn't have to be all or nothing, you know," he says.

"Have you met me? It's my mantra."

"More like an epitaph."

He's right. It's like I use one hand to push people away and the other to dig my own grave. I hate this about myself. But I'm not doing that with him. I'm trying. Can't he see that?

Lucas continues. "You can have everything, but not too much of any one thing. Balance in all things. That's what our coach always says."

The same coach who pressures his wrestlers to fast, binge, and purge in the name of winning? Lucas and his coach are both wrong.

"Is your coach the Oracle of Delphi?" I say instead.

"Huh?"

"Those are the words inscribed over the entrance to Apollo's temple in Delphi. He forgot *know thyself* and *surety is ruin* or a *pledge then ruin*; that one's more obtuse—"

"Oh my god, Gemma. Did you just make a joke? Or attempt to make a joke. You took the punch out of it with your long-winded explanation."

"Hey, I can be funny sometimes too you know."

"Sardonic. You can be sardonic. And sarcastic. And reticent."

"Okay, okay. Jesus."

"I'll tell you what else too. If this is the most fun you've ever had, we've got to step up our game."

I don't need to step up my game. I thrive on repetition and routine. On having too much of one thing.

When I was a kid, I always wanted to do my best days over. If we went to the beach, and it was low tide, and I found some kids my age to boogie board and catch sand crabs with, I'd beg to go back the next day and do it all over again. But the next day there'd be different kids, the tide would be high, and the jellyfish would be swarming. I learned too soon that days are like snowflakes not songs, no two are alike, and you can't play them over and over again. But I wish you could.

Despite my strong impulse to turn the car around and repeat every minute spent with Lucas in our wooded, Huck Finn-like hideout, I step on the gas and push onward.

"Fine," I say. "How many miles to Santa Claus?"

22

Santa Claus is a scam. A marketing ploy in a fur-lined velvet suit who pimps artificial happiness and drives retail sales. I was eight when I learned the truth. Riley McHenry called me a baby for still believing that a fat guy in red pajamas brought me presents once a year. "What other lies have you told me?" I remember my feigned indignation when my parents confirmed what I'd learned that day in Mrs. Smith's third-grade classroom from some snotty know-it-all as I stood in line to sharpen my pencil.

My parents donned somber, apologetic faces as they attempted to make the bitter truth more palatable and I soaked up the sympathy.

Secretly, I was relieved.

The idea that some guy was always watching me. That he knew when I was sleeping, and whether or not I'd been bad or good, was anxiety inducing. Like God. Except Santa showed up at your house once a year.

The mesmerizing highway lines slip between my hands poised at ten and two on the steering wheel. I crack the window to keep from falling asleep and glance over at Lucas. He's flipping through the brochures we picked up at the welcome center when we crossed into Indiana on I-64 about an hour ago. Chester is curled up on his lap.

"When did you stop believing in Santa Claus?" I ask.

He clutches his chest.

"There's no Santa Claus?"

I laugh. "Seriously. When?"

"Seriously. I have no idea. There was no big soul-crushing moment. I never discussed it with my parents. I just stopped believing. I probably heard it at school."

"Same."

"Were you sad?"

"To be honest, it weirded me out to think some guy in a red velvet suit broke into our house every Christmas Eve," I say.

"It was hardly a burglary. He brought presents."

I shake my head. "Didn't matter. My parents used to leave the front door unlocked because we didn't have a fireplace. That never seemed like a good idea to me. I should have figured it out sooner. There are so many holes in the Santa Claus story."

"Clearly, you were cynical even then?"

"It wasn't cynicism. It was fear. You know who scared me even more than Santa? The fucking Easter Bunny."

Lucas laughs. "Come on. You're kidding. The Easter Bunny?"

"Um, yeah. I mean, my only point of reference was that plastic-eyed overgrown rabbit at the mall. The thought of any animal that big wandering around my house hiding eggs." I shiver. "Why did they do that to us?"

"Let me guess. You hated Disney World too."

I gasp. "The most magical place on earth? Bite your tongue. I hope someone scatters my ashes in the waters of the Pirates of the Caribbean ride someday."

"You're a complicated woman," Lucas says.

Woman. I snort when he calls me that. I'm more girl than woman and I certainly wouldn't call Lucas a man or a boy. He's a guy. A bro. There needs to be a better word to describe a teen girl. Young lady or gal is something only a great aunt or grandmother would say. Personally, I'm okay with being called a girl for the rest of my life, like they do in *Cosmo* or Audrey Hepburn movies. I like the sound of the word. Its cuteness. It has nothing to do with not wanting to grow up, a trait all these asshole amateur psychologists like to assign to people with eating disorders. Rich, privileged white girls who never want to grow up. A gross and inaccurate oversimplification of a complex mental illness. It's like saying only people from certain ethnic or socioeconomic backgrounds can get brain cancer or some obscure autoimmune disease like the one that stole my mom from me.

My thoughts have pulled me deep inside myself. So much so that I forget where I'm going and that I'm driving.

"Right here. This is the exit!" Lucas yells and points. "Number sixty-three. Ferdinand, Santa Claus, Jasper."

When we get to the end of the exit ramp, he directs me to take South Main Street.

"It says here there are actually two post offices."

Lucas continues reading from *Your Guide to Santa Claus*.

"The official post office is at 45 Kris Kringle Circle. The only place in the world where you can mail a letter and get it postmarked 'Santa Claus.' The original post office, where we can write letters to Santa, is now a museum, with a twenty-five-foot statue of Santa in front."

I don't want to piss on Lucas's parade here, but what exactly is the goal of the Santa Claus postmark? Wouldn't letters from Santa be postmarked "North Pole" and why would Santa want to receive letters with his own name stamped on the envelope? Everything about Santa is bullshit.

"Where should we start?" Lucas asks.

I try to match his enthusiasm.

"Duh. With the twenty-five-foot statue of Santa, of course."

"It's so obvious now that you say it."

"Okay, so tell me where I'm going," I say.

"East Christmas Boulevard to Holiday Boulevard," he says without looking up from the guide. "Christmas Lake is surrounded by Candy Cane, Jingle Bell, Poinsettia, and Angel Lanes, Mistletoe and Madonna Drives. Oh, and the three wise men all have streets named after them."

"Apparently this town is replete with holiday-themed locations?"

"Would you have expected anything less?"

I wonder if that brochure mentions corn. Because despite all the clever street names?

Santa Claus is a fucking cornfield.

I hope we're not lured into its endless rows and murdered by creepy cult children. My more optimistic if not cynical self believes the kitschy town and theme park are a benign marketing ploy to attract tourists to the middle of nowhere. It would seem Santa, the man, and Santa, the town, have the same raison d'être. I'd be more annoyed at Southern Indiana if they hadn't also given us the childhood home of Abraham Lincoln. Like it or not, I will be dragging Lucas there next. It's only a few miles from here.

The giant Santa Claus statue sits on a grassy hill beside the Santa Claus church, built in 1880, and is surrounded by pre-Civil War-era town buildings including the historic original post office.

"We're going inside, right?" Lucas asks as I shift the car into park.

"Free admission? How could we not?" I say through a yawn. Faking enthusiasm is exhausting. "First, I gotta feed Chester."

Lucas groans. I shoo him away.

"Go walk around for a few minutes. I'll meet you by the entrance."

After struggling to feed Chester, who seems more intent on wearing the kitten formula than actually eating it, I accept defeat and tuck him inside my bag with a firm warning to keep his cute racoon lips zipped.

I find Lucas inside the old post office, which doubles as a museum and looks like a one-room schoolhouse. We sit in old-fashioned student desks and take the "tour" without leaving our seats, learning the town's entire history in ten minutes.

Santa Claus, Indiana, used to be called Santa Fee, but when the founders applied for their zip code, they were denied because it could be confused with Santa Fe. That's how they landed on Santa Claus, the only place in the US where letters from Santa are stamped with that special postal seal. The museum docent, Sue, rocks a pants suit and cap, and looks prepared to either deliver mail in 1947 or else conduct a train. She tells us Santa Claus, "the town not the man," (Sue's clearly a comedian) is home to the nation's oldest theme park, predating Disneyland by ten years.

"I'm pretty sure the ride pier at Coney Island, New York, dates back to the late 1800s," I whisper to Lucas who stops me from calling her out.

"Let her dream," he says. "Come on. Let's send letters to Santa Claus. The man."

"Be sure to include your return address, so Santa can write you back in December," Sue says. She hands us tiny pencils, the kind used for mini golf, and blank form letters that can be folded and stamped without an envelope. I move to check on Chester, concealed in the backpack on the floor between us, and Lucas shifts his back toward me.

"No peeking."

His pencil makes rapid scratching noises. What could he be saying? I sit. Stymied. This must be what it feels like to forget to study for a test. But when I finally touch my pencil to the paper, I ask for only three things, like Mom taught me, because that's how many gifts were bestowed on baby Jesus by the Magi. *We have everything we need, sweetie. Christmas is about giving to others.*

She was right then, just like she's right now. So, I ask Santa for three gifts. One is for Dad. One is for Lucas. And the last thing for myself.

That should keep the elves busy.

When we're finished, we staple our letters closed and buy two stamps from Sue. Lucas offers to drop them in Santa's special mailbox for us, where they'll be ferried away to the North Pole by magic.

On the way out, we ask Sue for directions to the nearest campground.

"Sorry, kiddos. You're not going to find a vacant campsite or cabin around for miles. Halloween is our second busiest holiday, with Holiday World holding its Fright Fest and all. People reserve spots months in advance."

"Very Nightmare Before Christmas," Lucas says.

Sue taps the point of her nose. "You got it. Chrismoween

I like to say." Then she pulls a pamphlet from the rack by the door and hands it to us. One hundred Things to Do in Santa Claus. "Here. There's still plenty of daylight and depending on which way you're headed, there's bound to be a motel with vacancies on the interstate."

Looks like that's our only choice. Either that or keep driving. I turn to ask Lucas which he prefers, but I've already lost him to the brochure.

"Obviously, we won't be riding the Thunderbird Steel Roller Coaster. Chester won't make the height requirement and we can't afford the admission. But there's ninety-nine other things to do," he says.

"Like what?"

"The Santa statue scavenger hunt. The archabbey and gift shop, Fat Daddy's Grill and Chill, Candy Castle…they have thirty-five flavors of cocoa!"

"At some point it stops becoming cocoa," I say.

"Hey, there's a drive-in movie! Double features are only ten dollars a car."

"Holiday movies?" I ask.

"Well, yeah. But there's eight screens. Got new releases too."

Two double features. Eight hours. Forget the overpriced no-tell motel on the interstate. This could work.

23

Jimmy Stewart's face glows on the big screen surrounded by the night sky and a billion other dead stars in the universe. It's a pinnacle scene in the movie. The one where Stewart's character in *It's a Wonderful Life*, George Bailey, grips the icy rail on a snowy bridge in Bedford Falls and contemplates plunging into the churning water below.

"Let me get this straight. The most beloved Christmas movie of all time is about a guy who attempts suicide on Christmas Eve?" Lucas asks.

We're wrapped in our sleeping bags and huddled together on the Impala's front seat. It's too cold to sit on the hood and even if we were allowed to keep the engine running for warmth, we can't afford to waste gas.

"Pretty much. The holidays are *not* the most wonderful time of the year for everyone," I say.

"I get it. But sometimes it helps to fake it until you make it."

What does he think I've been doing all day?

We'd spent the afternoon chasing Santa statues and Lucas's gastronomical interests all over this godforsaken cornfield. Rocky Road Fudge, giant snickerdoodles, pizza. It pained me, watching Lucas consume that much food and knowing he wouldn't give his body a chance to digest it. My thoughts flitted from worry for him, guilt, knowing I'd put Dad through the same thing, and a touch of envy, wishing I could join the party.

People like us aren't easy to be around. But neither are those who eat with reckless abandon because their metabolisms are fast enough to break the sound barrier. Like Zoe Peckinpaugh, who sat at my lunch table in ninth grade and scarfed down the school lunch of pizza or cheese nachos every single day without gaining an ounce and thought nothing of asking us how much we weighed. Was she really that clueless? Do such unicorns exist? Not in this car, they don't.

At any rate, the forced gaiety here in Santa Claus has tried my cold black soul, searing my olfactory glands with all things pumpkin and peppermint, and staining my retinal cones red, green, and orange.

George Bailey's tearful desperation in black and white is a welcome relief from the assault on my senses. I feel you, George. I feel you.

"I read Jimmy Stewart was actually crying when he filmed the scene in Martini's bar," I say.

"He's an actor."

"Yeah, but it wasn't in the script. He'd just returned from serving overseas during World War II. It wasn't George Bailey asking for help, it was Jimmy."

Show me the way, he'd asked God.

The cherubic Clarence answered George's plea, but did anyone show up for Jimmy? How about Monika? I don't remember an "angel second class" appearing in our hospital room. Someone to show her what life would be like without her. All she got was weekly visits from the psych squad, asking her if she had thoughts of suicide or self-harm. And me for a roommate.

I turn and put a hand on Lucas's arm. "Will you visit Monika with me when we get back? If she's not already in Colorado."

"Even if she is in Colorado. The furball is not invited."

Will the furball still be with me? I pull Chester closer and nuzzle him. Lucas shakes his head at my overindulgence, but I just smile at him. He rewards me with that chipped-tooth grin. The one I'm going to miss when our Thelma and Louise adventure ends. Because, who am I kidding, there will be no trips to Dillsburg for New Year's Eve or road trips to Colorado.

"Eventually we're going to have to figure out what to do with him," he says.

My smile goes crooked and my lungs feel like they're being squeezed. "Beeeeep!! Gemma's not here right now; please leave a message."

The right half of Lucas's face is illuminated by the movie screen, dividing it in two. Dark and light, good and bad. It's in all of us, but maybe not in equal measure.

He showed up for me, didn't he? And Monika and Declan showed up for both of us, and we showed up for Chester. So maybe the angels are winning after all.

I knew if I were drowning, you'd try to save me, Clarence says to George on the screen.

Is that what we're doing, saving each other? Or did I tie an anchor to Lucas's lifeline and drag him and a baby raccoon down with me? *If that's what you believe, then what are you going to do about it?* a voice inside me says. I can't blame Haymitch, I know it's my own.

I feed Chester as we watch. He takes ten full droppers of kitten formula before turning away, a mixture of sadness and concern in his increasingly expressive eyes. He's wondering how he's going to do it. Go on living without his mama. Me and this stupid eye dropper are a poor substitute.

I know that look.

Missing them doesn't get any easier. That's what I'd say to Chester if Lucas wasn't sitting right here. There are days when it's impossible to get out of bed because four tons of steel are pressing on your chest. And you'll have to learn how to suck back tears and hold them in until the middle of the night, when everyone is asleep, because people think grief comes with an expiration date and your sadness inconveniences them. Don't worry though. You'll figure it out. The breathing in and out part. The worse part is when you start forgetting to miss them.

I wave another full dropper under his nose. He turns away.

"Come on, little man, you need to eat more," I say.

My hypocrisy knows no bounds.

"I hope the little man you're addressing isn't me. But even so, I'm going to get popcorn," Lucas says.

My stomach rumbles.

"I'll come with you," I say.

I sense his relief at not having to decide if he should ask me if I want anything.

Outside, the wind has picked up, and I regret leaving my sleeping bag as we trudge toward the concession stand. It glows neon in the night, a beacon surrounded by pitch-black harvested fields. The perfect landing pad for extraterrestrials from a neighboring galaxy.

Inside the brightness blinds me. I squint until my eyes adjust. It's toasty warm and the freshly popped popcorn is intoxicating. My stomach stretches like a cat awakening from a long nap. "I'm starving."

Did I just say that out loud? One person's hyperbole is another one's truth.

Lucas orders the extra-large combo with a Coke while I peer into the candy case at the M&Ms, Jujubes, and ohmygod, they have Good and Plenty! Mom loved Good and Plenty. So did I. The white ones were her favorite. The pink mine. Popcorn was for movie nights, but Good and Plenty was for summer days at the town pool.

I glance at Lucas, hands in his pockets, bouncing on the balls of his feet.

"Anything else?" The cashier pans from him to me.

Vivi, so says the nametag, looks incredibly uncomfortable in her retro polyester button-down waitress uniform. Her cat-eye glasses are adorable and complete the look, but I can tell she's not exactly feeling those either. *Be the bright spot in someone's day*, Mom always said. Right after she let a car merge in front of her, bought coffee for the person behind her at Dunkin', or performed some other random act of kindness.

Lucas is about to tell Vivi he doesn't want anything more when I butt in. "Yes. I'll have two packs of Good and Plenty, a hot chocolate, and a small popcorn. Please," I say. "Nice glasses, by the way."

She smiles and touches the corner of her frames, adjusting them slightly. "Thanks, they were my grandmom's."

I nod appreciatively. "The real deal. Nice."

She gathers our order and rings us up. "That'll be $11.50." Then, sotto voice. "I only charged you for one box of Good and Plenty. They're a dollar at Walmart. Such a rip off here."

"Thank you so much!"

Look at Vivi, doing me a solid. I reach into my bag for money but Lucas waves me off.

I take my candy, peel open the top, and inhale.

I am six years old and standing on the high dive. There's a growing line of big kids behind me. Mom treads water below. *Jump, sweetie!*

I feel the rough surface of the board on my toes, the flip in my stomach as I push down, then spring up, arms flailing like a baby bird, but still flying. *I'm right here! I got you!*

I tilt my head back and pour the candies into my mouth. The sugary confection is sunshine and suntan lotion, endless daylight, and the weightlessness of freefall.

But then my toes hit the water and I panic. Gravity and inertia threaten to drown me.

It's too much. I'm choking. I scan for a napkin, a place to spit out the candy. *Relax. Don't fight it.*

Buoyant, I break the surface. Mom takes my hand and we paddle on our backs, staring at the hazy summer sky.

I breathe through my nose and swallow the candy-coated licorice tucked between my teeth and cheeks. *You did it! I'm so proud of you!*

By the time I reach the side, I'm ready to do it again.

Back at the car I polish off my box of Good and Plenty and popcorn. Belly full for the first time since leaving the hospital, I doze off halfway through the second double-feature, *A Christmas Story*, and fall into a sleep so deep, I dream for the first time in weeks.

Looks like Santa's been here! Mom squeals.

It's Christmas morning. The three of us are in matching flannel PJs. A green sparkle drum kit sits beside the tree. I grab the sticks and start banging away. I laugh. Dad, bleary eyed with bedhead, asks, "Drums? Did Santa think that was a good idea?"

Mom is beaming. "Of course *she* did!"

Because she was Santa. Mom died in January, midway through fourth grade. Looking forward to Christmas never seemed worth it after that. Not when I knew the shitty anniversary that was coming right after.

Boom, boom, boom, my tiny foot pounds the kick drum so hard, I wake up.

24

The thumping won't stop. It's coming from the other side of the frosty window. I press my warm hand against the glass until a spot clears and a red-cheeked female cardinal turns sideways and stares at me with one eye. Her gray plumes, tipped with red highlights in spots, lack the vibrancy of her crimson mate but she's equally as magnificent. Her beauty simply demands a closer look.

"Mom?" I say, because aren't cardinals messengers from the spirit world? She taps more emphatically. I cock my head and stare. "What's wrong?"

"Wake up, you two!"

The dregs of sleep dissolve from my eyes. The cardinal morphs into a burly dude in red Buffalo plaid.

"Come on. Let's go. To quote one of the great, underrated bands of my youth. Closing time! You don't have to stay home, but you can't stay here!"

I give Lucas a sideways slap in the arm and he startles awake. "Shows over. We're being evicted," I say.

"Uhh," he says like he's in pain.

Uhh, is right. I lay a hand on my distended stomach, cupping it like I've seen pregnant women do. Strewn around us are empty candy boxes and popcorn tubs, the remnants of our food binge. It's like waking up with a hangover in a stranger's bed after a one-night stand. I assume. Again, I have no knowledge of such things, but I can imagine the shame. I now understand Lucas's desperation to purge. But there's no time to ruminate on how to expel my transgressions and retreat into hunger. Not with Plaid Man giving me the stink eye.

He knocks again. "Come on. It's almost two in the morning."

He stands firm, watching me start the car and turn on the defrosters. Nothing but cold air blows out, turning the cold glass windows opaque. I rev the engine, check the gauges. I roll down the window.

"Warming up the engine. I can't drive if I can't see," I say.

"I'll get you some hot water," he says and walks away before I can stop him.

That's a terrible idea. The windshield could crack—I learned that from Dad, along with some valuable quick fixes for old cars.

"I'll check the trunk for an ice scraper," Lucas says.

I lay a hand on his arm.

"Can you pop the hood first? I want to try something."

When Lucas exits the car, I cut the engine, tuck Chester inside my jacket for warmth, and tear off one flap of his cardboard box. Outside our refrigerated cocoon, I notice for the first time we're the only ones left in the deserted drive-in lot. The giant screen and neon concession have gone dark, as have the stars, now covered by thick clouds heavy with precipitation. The scent of impending snow fills my nostrils when I inhale. I see my breath when I exhale.

Growing up, more than the equinox or solstice, the change of seasons was marked by the first day the furnace fired up after its summer slumber. I loved the *tick, tick, tick* of hot water filling up the baseboards and the smell of warm air wafting into each room. For the first time since we escaped, fear and loneliness touch me. Like icy fingers against my clavicle, they move up my neck, threatening to choke me. I wish I could teleport back in time to some First Day of Winter in the past, to the warmth and safety of my own bed with its worn quilt and oversized pillows, where I can turn over at first light and sink back into a deep sleep, before waking later to a guilt-free breakfast.

Sometimes I mourn that loss of the little girl in flannel PJs, sitting at the breakfast table on Sunday morning, eating Mom's buttermilk pancakes. Back before I feared food and was taught by others to be ashamed of my roundness. More elusive than Skinny, is a place where I'm loved and feel beautiful exactly the way I am. Or was. Those times, that girl, are gone, or else out of reach. Eden wasn't a real place either, was it? But a time before people were aware of our differences and the many cruel ways of pointing them out.

"Why'd you turn the car off, now it'll never warm up," he says.

He's already propped open the hood with the built-in metal support rock.

"It's never going to warm up inside the car anyway. Not unless I help it along."

I slip the cardboard behind the radiator, covering about three quarters of it, like I've seen my father do many times with his old Ford pick-up, the one he keeps saying he's going to restore when he has time. Who knew I was going to be such a handful? Lucas raises an eyebrow when he returns with an ice scraper.

"Sure that won't cause an engine fire?" Lucas asks.

It won't.

"Grab the leftover marshmallows just in case."

Lucas scrapes the windows while I start the car. I spend a few minutes applying steady pressure to the gas petal before trying the heater and defrosters again.

Thankfully, Plaid Guy is also Slow Guy. By the time he returns with hot water, the windshield and back window are clear, and the heat vents are blowing warm-ish air. I thank him and take the large Styrofoam cup from him before he does anything stupid.

"Did the weather forecast say anything about snow?" I ask him.

Lucas and I have been in a news/media void for almost forty-eight hours.

"Supposed to warm up here, but some artic air's blowin' in from Canada, gonna bring some early snowfall north of us. Up near Terre Haute and north of Indianapolis."

Great. Exactly where we're going.

25

I'm not sure when things turned bad for Chester. Not that they were ever good. But about two hours after we left the drive-in movie theater, crossed the state line into Illinois, and were heading north on Interstate 57, he let out a high-pitched chirp that emanated from deep in his belly and wracked his tiny body.

Lucas keeps trying to feed him, but he just turns his head and continues to scream. He hasn't stopped for thirty minutes now and Lucas and I, like first-time parents with an inconsolable infant, are rattled to the core.

"This the sound he made in the library?"

"Sort of, but this is much worse. At least then he stopped when I fed him. Why won't he eat? Do you think he's dying? Don't animals stop eating when they're dying?"

Lucas considers this. "I certainly hope not."

I'm in no mood for his innuendo.

"Maybe the formula has gone bad. I should have tried to feed him before we got back on the road."

"He was sleeping and we didn't have much of a choice. Don't beat yourself up."

That's like telling me not to breathe.

But Lucas is right. We'd gotten the boot from that cold, empty parking lot and needed to press on and cover some ground going northward toward Normal, Illinois, in case Plaid Man was right and we were driving straight into a freakishly early snowstorm. I stomp on the gas and grip the steering wheel harder.

"We need to find a vet," I say to Lucas.

He lays Chester in his box and squints out the window.

"Pull off at the next exit with a gas station. We'll fill the tank, ask around," he says.

Raisin-sized tears form in the corners of my eyes, blocking my field of vision and forcing me to blink in double-time to avoid a car wreck. I sense Lucas staring at me.

"You okay?" he asks.

"That lady back at the pet store was right. I'm not cut out to be a raccoon baby's mama. Listen to him. He's sounds like something hurts."

The silence from Lucas that follows makes Chester's keening more pronounced. My head buzzes and my hands go cold. Rivulets of tears run down my cheeks, join at my chin, and drip onto my sweatshirt. I'm a mess.

Lucas puts a hand on my shoulder and gently rubs my collarbone with his thumb.

"Hey, look at me. It's going to be okay."

I take my eyes off the road for a second to meet his gaze then snap my head back again. "Sorry," I manage.

"It's okay. I get it. You're attached. That happens more quickly under times of duress."

"That doesn't make it any less real," I say, in case we're no longer talking about Chester.

I exit the highway near Salem and pull into the first gas station we see and park beside the pump nearest the street.

"How many towns named Salem do you think there are in the United States?" Lucas asks as he hands me Chester and reaches for my road atlas.

I shrug. I don't have the energy for guessing games.

"I'm gonna check," he says.

"Knock yourself out."

Chester coils himself into a ball with his tail covering his eyes when I slip him under the bottom of my sweatshirt, creating a paunch like he's my baby kangaroo. I don't want to leave him inside the car alone while Lucas pumps the gas. He's still chittering, but he's quieting down, which does nothing to allay my fears that he might be dying.

The sun hasn't risen yet and in addition to a vet and a

restroom, I'm in dire need of a warm caffeinated beverage. But when I walk into the mini mart to pay, it doesn't have much in the way of amenities or sustenance, just a smattering of sodas and energy drinks, tobacco in all its forms, condoms, and lottery tickets. Perfect for a customer base that likes to take chances because, you know, condoms *are* only 80 percent effective and everything else here is addicting.

Is this the gas station for people with nothing left to lose?

Fitting, in a way. It seems I've been poised at the end of a craps table, clutching a pair of dice since we left the hospital. The time may have come for me to blow on them once for luck and let it all ride.

"I'd like twenty dollars' worth of gas please," I say to the woman behind the register as I slide the bill into the well under the teller-like plexiglass window, making me question the safety of working the overnight shift at a gas station right off the interstate.

She takes my cash, runs one of those pens over it to make sure it's not counterfeit, and flicks on the pump's switch without making eye contact. I almost lose my nerve, but I have to ask. This is for Chester.

"Hey, strange question, but would you happen to know if there's an animal hospital or emergency vet nearby?"

"Do I look like Google to you? Check your phone."

"I don't have one."

For the first time, she looks up, then cranes her neck around the counter to see Lucas filling the tank on our giant spotted car. I suppose our appearance elicits pity.

"You got a sick dog?"

I unzip my sweatshirt halfway, like I'm selling crack or stolen watches, and let her peek in at Chester, who's been oddly quiet since I stepped inside. I rest a finger on his belly to make sure he's still breathing. He is.

"Raccoon."

Her demeanor immediately changes as she succumbs to Chester's charms.

"Aw. Isn't she the cutest!"

I don't bother telling her that Chester is a "he." Don't want to spoil the mood.

"So, do you know of a place nearby?"

"Nope."

She snaps back to all business and walks away from the register, leaving me to believe I'm screwed, but just as I turn to leave, she calls out from the back. "Checking my phone!"

When she returns, she hands me an address written on the wrapper for Scott tissue. "This is about fifteen or twenty miles from here. Give or take." Then she nods at the camera mounted above the door. "Manager keeps an eye on us. No phones allowed. But this is an emergency."

"Thank you so much!"

"No worries. You be careful out there. You're awfully little to be driving a big old car like that."

I'm surprised and happy she described me as little. Because even now, that's what I want to be. I was worried my binge had ruined that. What would my fucking therapist have to say about that? Although now that I'm an escapee she's not really my therapist anymore, is she? That should give her something to flip her hair about.

"My brother's driving some too." Lying comes so naturally to me now.

"Where're you all headed anyway?"

I wave the toilet paper wrapper.

"Kinmundy animal hospital apparently. Then on to Chicago to visit colleges."

I lie in case the camera is recording sound as well as video.

"Thanks again."

"Godspeed," she says, making me think of Declan for the first time since we left the campsite. We should have let him know where we were really going. Just in case something happens. Even though it probably won't. Probably. Plus, if it does, there's not much he can do.

Back in the car, Chester can barely lift his head. When I

press the dropper filled with formula to his mouth, he wraps his hand around my finger and parts his lips, but then turns away. Like he's hungry and wants to eat but can't. I know how that feels, but now that I've witnessed it? There is nothing more heartbreaking.

26

It takes us longer than it should to find the animal hospital. How did humans survive for thousands of years without GPS? We made a few wrong turns before finding a pharmacy with a twenty-four-hour drive through, where we could stop and ask for directions.

Upon arrival, we discover not an animal hospital, per se, but a farmhouse with a free-standing cement garage out back that's been converted into an office. Unfortunately, it's shuttered closed at this pre-dawn hour but there's a light on in what appears to be the kitchen of the main house.

"Be right back," I say.

In a flash, I'm up the driveway, banging on a side door under the glow of a single porch light. I don't stop until I hear a disembodied voice. "We're closed. Don't open until eight a.m. There's an emergency vet in Louisville."

Chester can't wait two more hours.

"I'm sorry! There's no time to find someplace new. I'm not from around here and I think he's dying." I reach into my sweatshirt and cradle a limp Chester, swathed in Monika's sock. "See?"

The curtain on the door peels aside and the pinched face of a woman with salt-and-pepper hair appears. "Sorry, young lady. Raccoons aren't in my wheelhouse. I can get you the number of a wildlife expert."

Then she retreats again.

I keep banging. "Please!"

The inside door swings open and she cracks the storm door enough so that I see she's in a fluffy bathrobe. She peeks into the sock and sighs.

"Go on back to the office then. Be there as soon as I pour myself a cup of coffee."

Coffee. There's a longing in my chest. I tell myself it would be rude to ask for some and do as she says.

Fifteen minutes later, the three of us are standing around a metal exam table, with Chester curled in the crook of my arm. Dr. Burke, who has shed the bathrobe for blue scrubs, is not happy with us.

"He's severely malnourished and dehydrated. I'm going to start him on a drip of sugar water and then we'll see about getting some real food into him. He's going to have to stay here for a couple of days while I get him fed, vaccinated, hydrated." She sighs. "Folks have got to learn that wild animals aren't pets. It's best to leave them be. God knows how many times people unwittingly separate a baby from its mother."

My back goes up. "But his mother was dead."

Lucas jumps to my defense. "Yeah roadkill. We saw her."

"When and where was this?"

We look at each other, trying to come to some consensus with our eyes.

"Two-ish days ago?" Lucas offers.

"Ohio," I say at the same time.

"I'm not going to ask because it's none of my business, but that's a considerable distance and amount of time to be riding around with a sick wild animal. But he's here now and that makes him my responsibility. I'm going to get him well and get him back outside where he belongs. He's young. He's got a chance."

"He's not going to die?"

"Not likely. But if he went on this way much longer, he could have had a heart attack or kidney failure."

I know all this because I've heard all this. And that's all it takes for me to remember facts. Sticky brains are good for something.

"Because a starving body lacks potassium," I say.

"Where'd you learn that?" She cocks her head and reads me like I've got subtitles. Or worse, a newsfeed scrawling by under my chin, telling her my whole ugly backstory.

And in that moment, I realize I don't care. I'm so tired of pretending and protecting. Or denying. Or whatever it is that I've been doing for as long as I can remember to keep my story safe. It's not even a very interesting story and I realize don't want it to be mine anymore.

"During almost four weeks of in-patient treatment."

"For what?" she asks.

I'm anorexic, I almost say. But no, that's not right. That would be like saying, I am diabetes. And I'm not my disease. "I *have* anorexia."

The words are more cumbersome than a peanut butter-covered cracker in my mouth. It would have been easier to say, "I have *Ichthyophthirius multifiliis*," like my poor fungi-diseased fish at Just Pets.

I don't care if she judges me. I said it for Lucas and Chester and my dad who doesn't quite understand and has been asking himself "why?" and a mother who will never hear them. But her amber eyes are surprisingly kind. "Ah, so then you know that food is the best medicine for the severely malnourished and how delicate the process of refeeding can be." Then she touches me lightly on the upper arm. "And by the way. I'm sorry."

Lucas raises his hand. "I have bulimia. You might say the three of us have been running on empty."

"Lucas!"

"Too soon?"

Leave it to Lucas to joke about starvation in a way that makes the Donner Party seem like an actual party. I'm going to miss his comedic timing when this is all over, and it will be over soon. One way or another. This road trip is either winding down or unraveling. My gut tells me it's the latter and that scares me to death.

"How much will all this cost?" I ask.

She sighs and rubs her face.

"For care like this, it's about $150 a day. You're probably looking at about $600."

The terror on our faces must be evident because she is quick to amend.

"Tell you what, how about you give me what you can now and send me the rest later? I'll write you up a bill, but first, I'm going to take this little bandit in the back and get him started on an IV."

She puts out her hands to take him from me and pulls him closer.

"Can I have a minute to say goodbye?"

"Take your time," she says. "I'm going to get myself another cup of coffee."

"Um." I hesitate to ask, but she reads my mind.

"Cream and sugar?" It's not a question.

I nod dutifully, so grateful for her kindness, that I skip the part where I add up the fat and calories in my head. Baby steps.

When the vet leaves, Lucas takes Chester's tiny hand between his thumb and index finger and gives it a gentle shake. "Nice knowing you, buddy. I'm going to miss your stinky cheese breath."

All at once, I'm laughing and crying. Lucas puts his arm around my shoulders and holds me tight. I run my thumb from Chester's nose to the top of his head and back again until I hear Dr. Burke return. Before I hand him over, he plants his nose against my palm for a raccoon kiss and opens his eyes. *Thank you*, they seem to say. I kiss the top of his head in response. *The pleasure was all mine.* Only after I hand him over and watch him disappear through the door do I touch my nuzzled hand to my cheek.

27

S ixteen ounces. That's how much Chester weighs. I heard the doc "tsk" when the digital number popped up on the scale, saw her write it down on his chart. I know that sound. It's never good news.

"A six-week-old raccoon should be closer to nineteen or twenty ounces," she told us. Hmph. I thought raccoons weren't in her wheelhouse. Guess she consulted Dr. Google while she changed out of her PJs because she was shit full of information during his exam. Or maybe she explained it best when she said, "I've raised four kids, countless animals, and a husband. If I've learned anything, it's that so much depends on eating, sleeping, and pooping."

Turns out we should have been feeding him five or six times a day and holding him on his belly, not cradling him on his back like a baby. Oh, and burping him. His upper and lower GI tracts were full of gas.

Sigh. If only he'd farted, my arms wouldn't feel so empty now.

Instead, we're stepping outside carrying a bill for $587.22, a to-go cup with sweetened coffee, and two granola bars Dr. Burke insisted we take. No Chester.

"Snow," Lucas points out.

I heave once and choke back a cry. And tears. And everything else inside me that's been trying to claw its way out of the pitch black ever since it first occurred to me that my life would be better, that I would be better, if I were smaller. I turn now, like a slow-moving carousel, taking in the place where that desire, that obsession and the walls it created, has landed me.

A fine powder falls lightly from a creamsicle-colored sky, dusting the brown grass, the pavement, the Impala, everything, with a confectioner's sugar-like coating. Like French toast or powered donuts. Two old loves. But the tasty bucolic scene can't fill the Chester-sized hole in my heart or allay my fears about reaching Normal.

"Snow," I echo.

We're co-captains of the obvious.

My gut clenches. Now both time and weather are against us.

Lucas doesn't bother asking if he should drive; he just gets in and starts the car as I slide into the passenger seat, pull up my hood, and cinch it closed so I can't see. I hear them though, right before the engine turns over. I'd almost forgotten about them.

They slip into the backseat. Haymitch and Foxface. The invisible personifications of our respective eating disorders that we were forced to give names to back at the hospital. Up until now, they'd been silent passengers, but they're getting bolder, or worse, stronger. Whispering to each other like conspirators, plotting a mutiny.

Like I told Dr. Burke, I'm not my disease, but I gave it a life of its own and it's made me toxic. In an unintentional, innocuous way, like granite countertops or cell towers, emitting poison in small steady doses. But still.

What if Lucas left the hospital too soon and he's not medically stable? What made me think getting to a place called Normal was a good idea, or that I could save a fragile animal?

You can't even save yourself, one of them says. Probably Haymitch. Asshole.

"I know!"

"You know what?" Lucas is confused.

I don't bother explaining myself.

"Maybe we should turn back."

"We have less than 200 miles to go," Lucas says. "You are joking right?"

"Right?" he says again when I don't answer right away.

"Uh, yeah." I nod as I mumble through my hood. "Joking."

I don't have to see him to know he's scrunching his eyes like a confused little boy. Underneath his well-developed nonchalance he's been counting on me to get us to someplace better than where we started.

Time to pivot. Turn the conversation back toward the mundane so maybe he won't notice the fissures snaking along my carefully crafted shell. One big sneeze and I'm going to pieces.

"Less than two hundred miles, huh? I guess you've been studying the map. How many Salems have you found so far?"

"Too many. It's like there's one in every state."

"I wonder why."

"I know, right? Like I can see there being lots of Springfields or Milltowns, but what's the significance of the name Salem?"

I bite my lip, count backward from 100 to the metronome ticks of the wipers. Listen to the squeak of rubber hitting glass. Let one eye peak through a small gap in my hood. Goggle-like semi-circles have merged on the windshield where the snowflakes have been swooshed away. Lucas's hand enters my field of vision as he pushes the levers for the heat and defrosters on the dash. There's nothing but frigid air blowing, but I lack the desire and motivation to jump from the car and adjust the cardboard I placed behind the radiator. The sun is rising, and with it the promise of more warmth. I need to get the hell out of here already. I sense Chester in the building less than fifty feet away and Dad worrying from a distance at least three million times that. I exhale.

Eighty-seven, eighty-six, eighty-five…

Lucas put the car into drive and says, "Yeah, so back to all those Salems."

"Not the best idea for a themed road trip?" I offer.

"Depends on how much time we have."

The fact that he said "we" implies some nebulous future. Like somewhere in time there's some older version of us out there, in a future where we're both okay, better than okay, and we're *together*, sitting in side-by-side recliners, our pet raccoon curled up beside the fireplace, as we plan our road trip to all forty-eight contiguous states, and perhaps Alaska if our eyesight is still good and we're feeling extra adventurous. Because what's a little detour through Canada when you've got plenty of free time and gas money?

But then my thoughts go dark. Like they always seem to do. How much time *do* we have?

"Gemma?"

"Yeah?"

"I can sense you freaking out under there."

I loosen the strings on my hood all the way and turn so he can see my eyes.

"I think I should call my dad. Tell him what's going on," I say.

Has it really only been twenty-four hours since we left the campsite? What a mess. What a goddamn mess.

Lucas hands me the phone before finally putting the car in drive. "Try Dec first. We should know what we're facing. There could be an APB out on us for all we know. Like we're Bonnie and Clyde or— I can't think of any other criminal couples."

"The Rosenbergs?"

"Were they on the lamb? What does that even mean? The lamb. What do baby sheep have to do with running away?"

I know he's trying to make me laugh, and I love him for it, but a half grin is all I can muster.

I keep turning the phone over in my hands, happy to have something to hold while I decide what to do. For the first time in my life, losing a pound is painful.

28

Haymitch makes a move as soon as we're on the main road. I spot him in my periphery, about to throw one leg over the long bench seat and squeeze between us. I grab one of the granola bars from Dr. Burke, rip open the wrapper with my teeth, then take a bite to spite him, then slide into the middle spot before he gets there, close enough so that my shoulder touches Lucas's.

I hold up the phone beside his right ear, my left, and turn up the volume while the call connects.

Declan picks up on the third ring, his voice heavy with sleep. "Where are you?"

"Um, Salem?" Lucas offers.

"No, wait, Kinmundy," I correct.

"A state would be helpful."

"Of mind?" we ask together.

Declan exhales. "Actually, scratch that. I don't want to know."

"Where are you?" Lucas asks.

Declan laughs. "You have your secrets I have mine. What time is it anyway?"

"Eight," Lucas says.

"Seven your time," I say.

"You've become one of those old married couples that finish each other's sentences."

Silence.

"Hold on. Let me put some clothes on."

There's ruffling and a few grunts and groans. I blush, tilting my head away from the phone, while pressing my body closer to Lucas's.

"Okay, now I can think," Declan says.

Me too.

"Are you okay? I called like three times since last night."

"Fine," we say.

"Bro, listen. I'm sorry. Tomorrow's Monday. I won't say anything to tip him off but when my dad opens the junk yard—"

"Don't worry about it. We owe you. If he finds the car missing and reports it stolen, do what you gotta do."

"Okay. Whatever happens next. Just be safe. Both of you."

I think about our family vacations. How we'd always bring something back for our neighbors, the Manettis, Gus's family, to thank them for taking in our mail and watering our plants. A mug or napkin holder won't put a dent in the enormous debt we owe Declan. He put himself so far out there, and for what? So the two of us could throw a 1,500-mile cross-country tantrum?

Here's your miniature spoons from Kentucky, Indiana, and Illinois, Declan. Got a set for you too, Monika. Sorry we fucked with your lives.

"What should we do?" Lucas says when we hang up with Declan.

That is the million-dollar question.

Call our parents.

Turn the car around.

Go back to the hospital.

Go home.

Forget this happened.

Nope. I cinch my hoodie closed again and lay down on the front seat with my head resting on Lucas's thigh. I hear him swallow hard as he rests his arm against mine.

"Keep driving."

And we do, in silence, for the next half hour, until the snow starts to fall harder, and the roads get slipperier, and the wipers keep freezing up with big clumps of ice because the windshield is cold and my nose and hands are even colder. Eventually it becomes impossible to see and we're forced to pull off the interstate where we find a truck stop adjacent to a New Jersey-style diner and a Motel 6. Lucas pulls into a parking spot behind a row of tractor trailers.

"I'm sorry," I say.

"For what?"

"Roping you into this ill-conceived plan. Obviously, my starving brain didn't think this through."

"Whatever we did, we did together. You have nothing to be sorry for."

"Did?"

"Doing. We're still doing. Come on. Let's go inside. Get warm."

He moves to open the door. I clutch his arm and nod my head toward the motel behind us, which looks like the kind of place where people come to hide dead bodies and their illicit affairs. I'll settle for a warm shower and clean-ish clothes.

"Get us a table. I want to see how much a room costs," I say.

Lucas looks doubtful. "You sure? We can wait out the storm in the restaurant. If it's more than forty dollars, we can't afford it. We didn't count on the Impala sucking down gas when we came up with our budget. Maybe we can find a Motel 4 or 2. Do they have those?"

"I'm freezing and feel disgusting. I want to take a scalding hot shower, wash my hair."

I must smell like a giant raccoon by now. Probably we both do. It's like those litter box commercials where the people who live in the house have become desensitized to the smell of cat poop stinking up their foyer.

"Go ahead. Order me coffee. I'll be right there."

I wait for Lucas to fade from my view, then turn on the burner phone. Lucas and Declan have already put so much on the line. Time for me to put more skin in the game. Call in reinforcements before my dad calls out the National Guard, or the FBI, or whatever federal agency deals with missing children. I dial as I walk. It's the only way we'll be able to afford a hotel room and still have enough cash to get home. Calling the house phone of the last person in America without call-waiting or caller ID. Gram picks up on the first ring.

"Before you say anything, I'm fine. We're fine. Me and Lucas. And I'm so, so sorry for everything, but I need a big favor."

29

Coffee. Maple Syrup. Scrambled eggs. Toast. And bacon. I've stepped out of the snow and into the breakfasts of my childhood. My heart beats like a double-kick drum and my stomach roars like Mufasa from the *Lion King*. The noise almost drowns out the warning shots being fired from my brain.

I'm getting so tired of playing referee between my body and mind.

Lightheaded, I steady myself on the empty hostess podium, then spot Lucas at a window table. I take a tentative step, then serpentine between the packed tables between us and arrive somewhat breathless.

"All set. Got us a room."

Lucas looks up. "Yeah? We can afford it?"

"Turns out we're getting the Motel 6, for the price of a 4."

No need to mention my fairy grandmother, who cried when she heard my voice and agreed to call the motel and put it on her card. I've set into motion the catalyst in a chain reaction that might bring this trip to a more rapid conclusion, but I'm still betting we make it to Normal before the whole thing blows up in our faces.

I slide across the booth's leather seat without elaborating and thank him when I see my steaming coffee waiting. I try to peel back the lids on the little creamer cups, but my shaky hands won't let me.

I give up and rest my back against the seat. "It's been a minute since I've been in a restaurant," I say.

Lucas opens the creamers without me having to ask. I pour them in my coffee, then pick up the giant laminated menu. Its size and numerous selections scare me but I'm thankful for the coverage it provides. My eyes scan the pages but can't seem to settle on anything. It's too much, I can't do it.

Good girl, you shouldn't.

But we're starving! Every cell in my body cries in unison.

"I waited for you to order. Should I not have done that?" Lucas asks.

I gulp my creamy rich coffee, hyperaware of my taste buds coming to life, then call from behind my menu-turned room divider.

"It's fine. What looks good?"

"Are we ignoring rule number one?"

I picture the list we made that day in art class.

1. No talking about food. Ever.

I peek over the top. "Maybe we should revise the rules."

Lucas flattens my menu against the table.

"All of them?" he asks.

I'm wondering where his mind's at and if mine's right there with him. But the server descends upon us bringing with her a hurried energy. "Can I take your order?"

Thank you, waitress interruptus!

"I'll have oatmeal and a side of fruit," I say. My pre-hospital go to. Foods that can be rolled into napkins or remain unfinished without drawing too much attention.

"Pumpkin pancakes with a side of hashbrowns and sausage," Lucas says.

Mmm. I'm going to add that to my deathbed food list. My mouth waters. Around me animated voices rise and fall, silverware clinks against plates and mugs, the cook's bell dings. I hand my menu to the server.

"Actually, I'll have the same."

Fuck it.

"I'll put that order in right away."

Lucas keeps his eyes on me as our server takes his menu and leaves.

"You never answered me."

He leans in and lays both his hands flat on the table. Close to my side of the table. That's when I notice two V-shaped scars between the middle and ring fingers on both his hands. I trace the pinkish scar tissue with my index finger, aware that I'm initiating physical contact that may be construed as flirting.

"What happened?"

"That? I was born with webbed fingers."

"That's a thing?"

"Apparently. And a third nipple. My parents didn't know if they'd given birth to a baby boy or a nursing platypus."

I snort-laugh, then tilt my head, suspicious. I've already seen him bare-chested and nothing there looked peculiar, in fact, just the opposite. "Yeah, right."

His eyes widen. "It's true. Here, I'll show you."

He reaches to pull up his shirt, exposing his side up to his rib cage before I can stop him.

"Not here," I whisper-yell.

"What? Polythelia is no big deal. Lots of people are born with a third nipple."

I lower my voice and try to shush him with my eyes. "Would you please stop saying nipple?"

"Nipple, nipple, nipple—"

The server, a fresh pot of coffee in each hand, nods her head in my direction. "I'm with her, hot stuff. Keep your clothes on."

Lucas laughs and lets his shirt fall back into place. When she leaves he says, "There goes rule number two. I made you want me more, didn't I?"

He kinda did. Does this make me a cougar?

I shrug. "We'll see, Aquaman."

I wonder if it's a wrestler thing or jocks in general, but Lucas and Declan don't need much persuading to take their clothes off. I'd rather walk around in a chicken suit than have people see me naked, but his vulnerability makes me want to try, even if it's not in the literal sense.

"You know, I have a nipple story too."

Lucas mock gasps.

"And you've waited this long to tell me? Hold on, give me a second to mentally prepare myself. Then speak very slowly with a French accent if possible."

He's closing his eyes and pressing two fingers to each temple.

"Lucas, this is serious."

He drops his hands and folds them like an obedient kindergartner.

"I'm sorry. Continue."

"When I was ten years old, I showed up at school in this lightweight, see-through T-shirt that did little to contain my burgeoning braless boobs," I begin.

Lucas's eyes widen but our plates arrive before he can say anything. They smell amazing—cinnamon, nutmeg. Most people don't know that pumpkin flavoring has nothing to do with the flavor of pumpkin. I smear butter across the top of my steaming pancake stack, dissect it into pieces, and take a bite. Ohmygod, it's so good. Unlike the food I was forced to eat in the hospital, which mixed with the acrid flavor of resentment in my mouth, I give in to its warmth and deliciousness.

I keep talking while I eat, which makes both easier—the telling and the eating.

"My teacher sent me to the nurse like I'd done something wrong. She said I was a distraction," I say.

"Maybe the real distraction was all the fifth-grade boys with hard-ons."

I laugh, which helps me share for the first time the more painful details that I've unpacked and repacked so many times I've begun to doubt them, like those old road maps that fit in the glove compartment. The more they're opened and refolded the less chance there is of aligning the creases just right.

I remember sitting in the nurse's waiting area, perched on the edge of that orange plastic chair, arms shielding my chest, and paralyzed with humiliation. A second-grade boy in a Mario Bros shirt was coughing beside me, there was a girl my age there icing her knee, and a boy on crutches who came in holding a hall pass. From behind the tall counter the nurse phoned my dad, telling him in a stage whisper that everyone could hear to bring me a sweatshirt to cover up and that I really should be wearing a bra.

"Kids were already teasing me about being fat at this point," I say. "I didn't think it could get worse."

We're not born hating our bodies. I didn't know what was wrong with mine until a bunch of fifth graders and a callous school nurse pointed it out.

"Some people shouldn't be allowed to work with children," Lucas says.

"That's what my dad said when he got there! He let her have it. Then he pulled me out of school for the rest of the day, which I loved him for. I would have enjoyed it a lot more if we hadn't stopped by the mall on the way home to buy bras."

Lucas winces. "I'm so sorry."

"I know!"

"It couldn't have been easy for him either. In his defense, he's just a guy."

Lucas is right. Poor Dad. We both got tossed into the rough waters of puberty without Mom there to navigate. It was the first time I remember getting angry with her for dying, for leaving me with the indelible memory of the day I lost my father too. Because we couldn't be pals after that. The day my stupid breasts arrived, two interlopers who came between us, making me self-conscious about being hugged by him or anyone else. Or dressing in a way that would ever again call unwanted attention to my protracted mammary glands, which isn't easy given the options we're fed by influencers. Finding a cute one-piece bathing suit that's not made for competitive swimming or moms is impossible for girls. Boys are so lucky that their penises aren't in a perpetual state of erection or that society and the fashion industry haven't deemed ballet tights the "must have look" in sexy attire.

"Thank you. I never thought I'd be able to laugh while telling my fat-girl-with-big-boobs story."

He stabs a stacked wedge of pancakes and points the full

fork at me. "I can't speak to the big boobs, but I was a fat kid too. I figured out quickly that cracking jokes, especially the self-deprecating variety, kept kids from making fun of me."

I frown. "That was a lot to put on yourself. You shouldn't have had to do that."

"Maybe not. Probably not. But being the funny fat kid was better than being Lucas Lard Ass. It turned out okay. Look at me now? I'm a freaking god."

Is he a god or is he Sisyphus? Forever pushing a boulder uphill. I mean, look at where we are. One struggling to finish breakfast, the other struggling to keep it down. I look around, jealous of the people in this diner who can eat with ease, without thinking about it. And why shouldn't they? Humans need food and have every right to enjoy it. It's at the center of all cultural rituals, weddings, holidays, funerals. But I can't imagine a day when every bite isn't seasoned with guilt.

"Normal seems unreachable," I say to Lucas.

Outside, the snow comes down sideways, like rain. Tenacious white crystals clinging to everything they touch and turning the world to ice.

"It's got to end eventually, right? We're so close."

I turn from the window. His pupils look like two tiny black dots in the blinding white sky. I imagine mine must too.

"What if it gets worse before it gets better?" I ask.

He holds my gaze as I hold my breath, waiting for reassurance. But then he throws his napkin on his empty plate and motions toward the restroom. "I'm gonna—"

I hesitate for a second, a cold mix of disappointment and betrayal clouding my thoughts, before grabbing the check off the table.

Maybe he thought I was talking about the weather. Either way. I got my answer.

30

It's colder in our motel room than it is outside. Seriously. I can see my breath. Despite my fiddling with the thermostat and controls on the combo heating/cooling unit, it won't turn on.

"Think your cardboard trick will work on that?" Lucas asks.

His eyes dart around. I watch them land on the TV remote. I'm losing him.

"HVAC is beyond my capabilities."

He presses a few buttons as he points it at the flatscreen bringing it to life.

"ESPN," he says.

He's lost. I don't do sports.

"Let me find out what's going on," I say, though I doubt he heard me.

At the front desk I learn there's also no hot water.

"We're working on it," says front desk woman.

But she tells me the laundry room is fully functional and available as long as I'm washing in cold. So as my dreams of a hot shower slip away, I return to the room to gather our dirty clothes and collect stray quarters.

I call to Lucas who's in the bathroom brushing his teeth, warning him about the hot water, or lack thereof, and letting him know I'm leaving to do laundry. I get a garbled reply before I hear him spit, which annoys me. Or maybe worries me is more accurate. Bulimia wreaks havoc on teeth. The constant splattering of stomach acid on enamel causes tooth decay, gum disease… He's headed toward a life of early dentures. If either of us make it that far.

"What?" I call.

The bathroom door opens and he hands me the clothes he's

been wearing for twenty-four hours, or is it thirty-six? I've lost count.

"I tucked my undies in the pant leg," he calls from behind the door.

"What is it with wrestlers and your proclivity for nudity?" I ask.

Years of changing for gym class has turned me into Harry Houdini. I can undress and dress without anyone so much as catching a glimpse of my bra or panties.

"Have you ever seen our uniforms?" Lucas answers. "Lycra singlets that leave little to the imagination."

Huh. My interest in sports has been piqued. Wrestling, at least.

Outside I follow the signs for the laundry room toward an alcove under the cement staircase, which also happens to be where the vending and ice machines reside.

One of my jobs when I was a kid on family vacations was to fill the ice bucket that sat beside the shrink-wrapped plastic cups on the vanity in our motel rooms. I was obsessed with ice machines. Pushing that lever, secretly filling and dumping the bucket several times before returning to our room with the half-moon shaped cubes.

"The ice lady cometh!" Dad used to joke.

Years later I figured out the corny Dad joke was an allusion to Eugene O'Neill's maudlin play, but it made me and Mom laugh, and that was the point, wasn't it? That and giving me a special job, unique to family road trips, like the travel-sized laundry detergents, shampoos, and cereal boxes that only emerged on vacations. Sure, you *could* buy pint-sized Frosted Flakes any time of the year, but it wouldn't be the same.

One of the dryers is running on high when I walk in, filling the air with warmth and the scent of lavender dryer sheets. I quickly shut the door behind me to seal it all in. On the floor beside the folding table sits a plastic storage container with "Lost and Found" written in Sharpie on the lid. With no one there to see, I take the opportunity to rummage through it and

find an extra-large flannel, an assorted pile of socks with no
mates, leopard print leggings, kids pajamas, and a black Lycra
dress. I throw everything except the kids' jammies in with our
wash and am trying to figure out how to insert dollar bills into
the machine when the door bangs open.

"Oops, sorry, hon," says a woman carrying an empty laundry
basket. "Hope I didn't scare you."

She gets right to the task of emptying her dry clothes into the
basket, then turns to me, holding out the box of dryer sheets.

"Need one?"

I pull one from the box.

"Thank you."

"Sure thing. You be safe out there. It's getting nasty."

I peek outside. The brightness makes me squint. The parking lot is smooth white, no tire tracks or blacktop in sight, and
the snow is still falling. I thought this was a pit stop to eat, get
clean, and rest up for a few hours, but if it doesn't let up, I guess
we're staying the night.

"You too, be safe," I say, then turn back to my washer and
run my finger along the touch screen to search my washing options. That's when I see it. Right between *heavy duty* and *delicate*.
Normal. Huh. When I press the word, a green light goes on. The
effortlessness is not lost on me.

Back at our room, Lucas has managed to create a tent bed,
reminding me of the *Curious George* variety I had when I was
little. I loved my secret hideaway perched atop my twin bed and
slept in there longer than most kids should. Inside, Lucas is
hunkered down, sans clothes, in a sleeping bag watching ESPN
through the propped-open flap. I pull the newly acquired flannel from the pile then climb inside to give it to him.

"It's still warm," he says, burying his face in it. "And it smells
so good."

Evidence of how badly we must smell. The front desk lady
promised to call our room when the heat and hot water returned.

"Don't hate me but I stole it from the lost and found."

"You know that's where I shop."

I laugh. "Nick's wrestling sweatshirt, right."

My stomach twists thinking about what this trip is costing him.

"Yep, for Kaitlin it was all about the jacket," he says.

High school and all its arbitrary rubrics by which we measure a human's worth.

I climb through the tent opening and sit, crisscross apple sauce, on the bottom of the bed. "That's how I felt about my boobs. They were the main attraction, not me."

They turned a little girl into a woman before she was ready. Someone may as well have handed me, I don't know, a loaded gun? An abacus? I was equally clueless about what to do with those.

"They made me bigger in every sense of the word. Drawing attention from gross old men. Forcing me to go up two sizes in shirts and dresses. I wanted to be smaller. Needed to be smaller. Skinny. That's what I was looking for in my road atlas. It became a place I needed to get to."

"You mean like Los Angeles?"

I manage a half-hearted smile and think of the imaginary destination I'd conjured, where thighs didn't touch, and double D boobs shrank to AA-ville. A place where I'd feel comfortable inside my own skin.

"In retrospect that might have been a more direct trip."

My body goes cold. The heat I soaked up in the laundry room has escaped my skin cells. Craving warmth and coverage, I crawl to the top of the bed and tuck into the sleeping bag beside Lucas's.

Lucas turns to me, invading my personal space, as I situate my head on my pillow.

"I'm sorry. I shouldn't joke," Lucas says. His words sound slurry.

I inhale.

"Have you been drinking?"

"Nope."

"Are you lying?"

"Yes." He pulls a flask out of the sleeping bag. "Whiskey. For emergencies."

Declan.

"Whiskey won't keep us from freezing to death," I point out.

"True. But we'll be happier about it." He takes a sip and hands it to me. "Here. It will keep you warm. Or…it will make you *believe* you are warm."

I hesitate, but not too long, before I take the flask and raise it up in a toast. "Salute."

To our health! And me. For all the high school parties and whatever other rites of passage I've missed. May this be the first of many points shaved off my Rice purity test.

I take a gulp, hold it in my mouth for a few seconds, and let it slip down my throat. Immediately, heat flows down my esophagus, spreads throughout my chest, and deep into my core. I'm on fire. In a good way. Lucas watches for my reaction and reaches for the flask, but I turn my head and take another sip.

"This," I say, "is magic."

"You've been holding out on me, Leonardo," he says, taking the flask back.

I raise my hand in a pledge. "First drink ever, I swear. Except for sips of wine on holidays 'cause you know, Italian."

"Cin cin." Lucas offers anther Italian toast before taking a swig.

I lay back and sink into the lumpy bed and the warmth generated by the whiskey, the closeness of Lucas's body, the greenhouse effect of the tent. My muscles relax and the chatter in my brain goes quiet. Fuck meditation.

"Somehow I didn't picture you as a whiskey drinker," I say.

"I prefer weed, actually," Lucas says.

I turn, propping myself up on a bent elbow and give him a hard stare. It's possible I'm a tad dizzy.

"What?" he says. "It's legal in a lot of states and less harmful than alcohol."

"For fully developed brains."

"I assure you. My brain is *highly* developed. Which is why I prefer weed to alcohol."

He makes a good point. Plus, who am I to preach about the ill effects of controlled substances on the brain? I starved mine (the brain needs at least eight hundred calories a day), forcing it to shut down all functions unnecessary to immediate survival—menstruation, hair growth, blood flow to my extremities. When I met Lucas, I had only recently begun firing on all circuits again.

"Doesn't keep you warm, though," I say.

I hold out my hand for the flask.

"Uh-uh. I don't want your judgement impaired."

I wave my hand.

"Let me present our current situation as evidence that I have no judgement to speak of. Plus, it's not like I'm operating heavy machinery. Come on."

I reach for the flask again and he tucks it into his sleeping bag.

"Don't think for one second that your nakedness will deter me from reaching in there."

He tilts his head, as if weighing his options.

"Nope, sorry. I need to ask you something first."

"Fine. Ask. We'll stick a pin in my impairment."

Lucas looks so serious, I'm suddenly shy about meeting his gaze, so he touches his forehead against mine, making it impossible to look away.

"Can I kiss you?"

I love that he asked first.

I nod yes. He presses his lips to my forehead and slides a hand along the side of my face. My heartbeat sounds like miniature marching soldiers in my ears, *chu, chu, chu*... I close my eyes and turn my mouth up to meet his. It's a deeper kiss than the one we shared at the campground. His hand moves between my shoulder blades and I feel my heart through my rib cage and spine, pressing against his hand as he presses me to his chest. I'm contemplating things that would surely complicate an already complex situation when the phone rings like a fire alarm. For the hearing impaired. I jump and our teeth collide and I bite my lip. "Ouch!"

I roll toward the nightstand and fumble to lift my side of tent so I can grab the phone. For some reason, I think it's my dad. I've been expecting to hear from him ever since I phoned Gram. Plus, I wouldn't put it past him to know when his daughter's reputation might be on the line.

"Hello?"

Front desk lady announces herself. "Hot water's back. Get it while you can," she says.

I roll back to face Lucas and tell him what she said. I'm torn, but not really. I think of the black Lycra dress, the clean smell of soap, freshly washed hair. I'd like to look my best before picking up where we left off.

"I really need a hot shower."

Lucas looks disappointed. "Save some water for me."

I scooch to the end of the bed and out the tent opening. Before I can change my mind, I pop my head back in.

"You can come with me?"

He blushes. His expression reads like a row of question marks followed by a row of exclamation points.

"Is this the whiskey talking?" he asks.

I shake my head. It most definitely is not. This is something I want and need to do, in case there's no future for us, separate or apart, and I go the rest of my life without meeting another Lucas. I've already been turned inside out and stripped bare before him.

"I want you to see all of me."

Because it's the only way I'm going to see myself. I hope that's what my eyes say in the intense quiet that follows.

Then I walk away, uncertain but determined to appear confident.

In the bathroom, I turn on the water and take off all my clothes. The full-length mirror on the door affords me the opportunity to preview what Lucas might see. I don't remember the last time I saw myself naked and have to fight the urgency to turn away before taking inventory. Hair check. Boobs check. Hips, butt, knees. Check. I'm not going to lie. It's a struggle. Stifling the haters' voices, my own included, while straining to hear any signs of movement on the other side of the door. Hearing none, I pull back the curtain, step into the shower, and pray that as the water sprays my face, that I will dissolve into oblivion and seep down the drain like primordial soup and get swept into the waste stream so as to avoid the humiliation awaiting me outside this door.

I'm such an idiot.

But then there's a click, a rush of cold air, and Lucas's voice.

"Prepare to be amazed," he says.

I laugh, a mixture of nerves and relief.

I already am.

31

The retching wakes me from a dream. The one where this guy and girl run away together and instead of one or both of them dying, they live happily ever after. It's a nice dream, and I'm trying to get back there, but I can't push past the flushing toilet, the running water, the toothbrush scrubbing, and the spitting, to the warm water and kisses, the anticipation and then excitement of each other's touch.

Skinny can be ugly.

The bathroom door opens and I play possum. I'm good at it, after all. *The best, baby.* Haymitch says. *Don't listen to those idiots. Just keep doing what yer doing.* He's slurring his words. He must be drunk.

Lucas slips back into the tented bed beside me and drapes his arm around my waist. I lean into him and we meld together, a pair of empty, tarnished spoons.

"To be clear—" Lucas begins.

"We're not having sex," I say.

"Had to ask."

"Noted."

Lucas laughs, but I'm distracted. Post shower, before eventually falling asleep, me in my pilfered Lycra dress, Lucas in his underwear (of course), we watched *SpongeBob* (his choice not mine), the Weather Channel, and *Dateline* (my choice not his) while binging on vending machine snacks. (Pop Tarts taste better with whiskey. Everything tastes better with whiskey. Who knew?) We also counted our money, the miles left to go before reaching Normal, and the number of times we'd need to refill the gas tank to reach home, and agreed to wait out the snow and push onward.

Sticky brains must finish what they start.

Problem is, we didn't finish what we started back at Children's Hospital. Now we've started something new between us, which complicates everything. The stops, the starts, the miles gained, and ground we lost. I tuck the covers under my chin. Everything feels off-kilter. It's possible I'm hungover.

It's late afternoon. Golden-hour sun slips through the slit where the curtain panels don't quite meet. The room is warmer, the snow has stopped, and there's still some daylight left. But the thought of what's waiting for us on the other side of that door, of everything we stand to lose, squashes my urgency to move.

"You okay?" Lucas talks into my hair.

"I've been thinking."

"Okay."

"You weren't at the hospital as long as I was."

He stiffens. Maybe because I did first.

"And—"

I don't know why I pick now to say it. Perhaps it's his minty breath, upbeat oblivion, or a stark realization that this ride we're on is a carousel that never stops or gets anywhere, only now it's speeding up and one or both of us may get thrown from our jeweled horse.

"I'm trying to remember. You said they transferred you from cardiology to our unit?"

He uncoils from me and lies flat, hands behind his head.

"Your unit," Lucas says. "Where are you going with this?"

His sharpness stings. I sit up and look at him.

"Well, what did the doctors say? About your heart, I mean."

"When did this become about me?" he asks.

In a flash, he's out of bed and pulling on a sweatshirt and jeans before I have time to register his anger and my hurt.

"It's always been about both of us."

"I'm not the one starving myself, Gemma. You're the one who almost passed out."

I crawl to the edge of the bed so I can see him better and sit back on my legs.

"Right. I'm the only one with the problem?"

"Aren't you? You're the one who wanted to get to Normal so badly. I told you back in Kentucky. This wasn't about some symbolic road trip to cleanse my psyche. I'm fine. I just wanted to get away from that hospital. I didn't belong there."

"Neither did I!" I'm shouting.

"I eat." He emphasizes the second word.

"It only counts if you digest."

"All wrestlers cut weight."

"Lose. You lose weight like the rest of us."

"Cut. Lose. Whatever. I can stop at any time."

"Stop what?"

I challenge him to answer. Wrestlers have the best pro tips for quick weight loss; I've done my research. Among other tricks of the trade, they drink two gallons of water daily, then dehydrate themselves two days before a match to make weight. Lucas knows that's not what I'm talking about.

"Purging. Is that what you want me to say? Does it matter? I'm still in control of my body."

Not the C word—oh no, he didn't. I live my life in a constant state of restraint.

"Do you know how much control it takes to live on water and one apple for three days?"

"Anorexia trumps bulimia? That's what you all think anyway, am I right? Here's a better question. Why would I want to live on an apple for three days? Why would you?"

His words are like punches. The kind that leaves ugly bruises. I jump out of bed and assume a fighting stance. "Are you asking or taunting? Why would you say that?"

"Because I really want to know. My best chance at a scholarship is to wrestle as a lightweight. I have a good reason to do what I'm doing."

"Oh, for fuck's sake, take out loans like everybody else! My reasons are as good as your sorry ass excuses."

"What good reason could you possibly have, Gemma? You're smart and sweet and beautiful. At any size. Just like your mom."

I clench my fists so hard my nails break the skin on my palms. My mom fought so hard to live. I'm not like her at all.

"We're not talking about me or my mom. I was trying to talk to you about your bulimia. I'm worried you weren't medically stable when we left the hospital."

"I don't have bulimia."

"You told the vet you did."

"I was *joking*. Trying to break the tension after your big confessional. You have to admit, it was awkward. Guys don't have eating disorders."

Except they do. He heard the same stats as I did at the hospital. At least a third of everyone with disordered eating is a guy. More probably. Eating disorders often go undiagnosed if someone doesn't fit the misguided, grossly inaccurate stereotype. His feigned ignorance stings. If it's denial, then it's alarming.

I close the gap between us, get up in his face and scream.

"Don't you dare do that!"

I've never been so close to hitting someone. He takes a step back.

"Don't do what? What am I doing?"

"Making me feel like a weirdo. Shaming me. You want to know why I wanted to be skinny? I wanted people to like me. I wanted them to love me. *I* wanted to love me."

His body softens and my breathing slows as we stare at each other for an eternity, saying nothing.

"Come on, Gemma, you are *so* loveable. Your problem is you push everybody away."

He moves toward me, arms open, and attempts to pull me in for a hug. I give his chest a slight shove and he backs away. He clenches his jaw and I sense him fighting his wrestler instincts to sweep my legs out from under me and pin me to this worn-out carpet. But then he turns his back on me and walks away.

"I don't need to push that hard, do I?" My voice chokes with tears.

I grab frantically for my clothes strewn across the floor and the chair beside the bed, not caring anymore which are clean or dirty, or that I'm full-on ugly crying with sobbing, heaving, running snot. This is what happens when I get too close. I'm like a glass cactus people think they can hold onto until they feel the prick of my needles and drop me to the floor where I shatter.

"Gemma," he implores.

I stomp toward the bathroom.

"I'm going to get dressed. Why don't you pack the car so we can get the hell out of here already? I just want to go home."

"What about Normal?"

"Forget, Normal! There's no such thing. That day in art class, I should have told you I was thinking of road tripping to Narnia. Then you would have seen me for the fucking lunatic I was—am. And you would have run away without me."

I slam the door behind me with a ferocity that hurts my bones.

The roads are plowed clear and framed with snow drifts, but the salted pavement is still slippery with patches of black ice. The world would look pretty through someone else's eyes.

"Gemma, slow down. You're driving too fast. Do you even know where we're going?"

"Home. I told you."

The front seat is crowded with Haymitch and Foxface wedged between us, laughing. They knew we'd never make it. Our bodies rule our minds, not the other way around.

"Come on, I'm sorry. We came all this way. Turn the car around. Let's go to Normal like we planned."

He reaches toward me, and I think he's going to grab the steering wheel, so I jerk my hands to the left, away from him, and that's when the car starts to fishtail, sending us down a wormhole where time and space stop and speed up simultaneously. What was it my driver's ed teacher said about this? Do I turn into the spin, do I pull out of it? Pump the breaks? It doesn't matter. The car is so big, physics takes over. There's no fancy computer chip to autocorrect the mess I've made. All I can do is watch as we career off the road and into a snowy embankment. When we finally stop, I'm too numb to move or speak. We both just sit there catching our breath.

"Are you okay?" Lucas asks.

I nod.

"I'll check on the car," he says.

To avoid stepping into the mound of snow, Lucas climbs into the back seat and out the driver's side rear door. I rest my forehead between my hands, which are still clutching the wheel at ten and two. No air bags in this ancient automobile. The door swings open again.

"We got lucky. There's no damage that I can see. Give it some gas and see if you can straighten the car and pull out of here."

I exhale. "Lucas, I'm—"

He holds up his hand. "Let's focus on getting Declan's car back on the road. You're right. It's time to go home."

Then he slams the door. It sucks, sometimes, getting what you want. I gun the engine again but the back tires spin without gaining traction.

"Stop! Put the car in park," Lucas yells from behind the car. "Can you pop the trunk?"

I can't find a button inside, so I get out of the car and use the key, then stand there, numb, as I watch him rummaging around until he finds whatever it is he's looking for. He emerges with Chester's flattened, poop-stained box and the sight of it immediately makes my eyes tear. I don't know why we kept it, but I guess it's good that we did. He digs in the snow with his hands, then wedges it under the stuck rear tire.

"Okay, put the car in drive again. Wait for my signal, then apply slight pressure to the gas."

Lucas's hands are bright red with cold. It pains me just to look at him. But I roll down the window so I can hear him and hope it works so he can get back in the car and I can apologize. Convince him I was wrong. That we should get back on the road to Normal.

I do as he says. The first two times the Impala rocks forward but doesn't budge.

"Okay, hold up!"

He walks alongside the car toward me, arms wrapped around his torso. Now all the color has left his face and he's sweaty.

"I'm going to get behind the car and push."

"Lucas, come on. You're freezing. Take a break."

He shakes his head. "It's almost out. We can do this."

I watch Lucas in the rearview mirror as he gets into position and yells, "Go ahead!"

I put my foot on the gas and pop! Just like that, the Impala is unfrozen. "Woohoo!" I yell, genuinely elated. I glance in the rearview mirror expecting to find Lucas cheering with me but see only snow and sky.

"Lucas?" I call out.

I shift into *park*, open the door, and step out far enough to see behind the car. Lucas is splayed out facedown like a backward-facing snow angel. At first, I'm relieved, thinking he's joking. Because we were fighting and that's what Lucas does to make things better.

"Come on, Lucas! That's not funny. Quit joking. You're going to freeze. Lucas?"

When he doesn't move, I race toward him, slipping and sliding, and crash to my knees on the ground beside him. I place my hand between his shoulder blades, and feeling no movement, I flip him over gently and check his neck for a pulse. Nothing. The skin around his mouth is blue.

"Lucas!" I tap his cheek lightly. "Oh my God, Lucas! Can you hear me?"

I part his lips, sweep his mouth with my index finger and prepare to do CPR but then think to call 911 first. I pat down my pockets for the phone and come up empty.

"Fuck!"

Realizing it must be in the car, I jump up. Slip and fall to my knees. I crawl toward the rear bumper and grip the cold metal as I pull my legs under me and steady myself to stand. With the car as support, I gain enough traction to sidestep toward the rear door, pull on the handle, and launch myself into the backseat. Breathing heavily, I scour the seats and the floor and come up empty. Reversing course, I slide my way to the ground beside Lucas and dig around in his pockets. I find it in his front pocket, punch in 911, cradle it between my neck and chin, then begin chest compressions while screaming I-don't-know-what at the operator who stays on the line with me, despite the fact that I'm incoherent and not all that sure they're helping me to help Lucas. That's when I cry out for the person I want and need the most.

"Mom!" I scream in frustration. "Help me! Please! Can you hear me? Don't let Lucas die too. Please, Mom?"

My frozen interlocked hands pump harder. I close my eyes and count, unable to stand the sight of Lucas like this. *One, two, three, four, five. Breathe. One, two, three, four, five. Breathe.* His stillness, the silence, pierces my soul. But I keep pumping, and counting, and breathing for both of us until there are sirens, and lights, and hands on my shoulders pulling me from him. I shirk them off, cradle Lucas's upper body against me and rock, begging him over and over not to leave me, while they slip him out of my arms onto a gurney and lift him, lift us both it seems, and carry us to the back of an ambulance, where they strap me into a seat so I can see but can't touch him as they continue CPR and ask me all kinds of questions a stupid genius like me should know the answers to. Name, age, addresses, contacts numbers, what happened... I fumble with my words, not getting the right answers out fast enough. I'm drowning, surfacing for seconds at a time, before plunging into darkness again, and then, right before everything goes still, someone says, "We have a pulse."

32

S ound erupts again when we pull up to the emergency entrance at Bloomington General. The bay doors open and two EMTs jump from the truck to catch a moving gurney with Lucas on it. They take him away from me before I have a chance to process what's happening. Then someone in scrubs ushers me to a waiting room and when my head and the room stop spinning, I realize I'm still holding the phone.

My thumbs punch in the phone number without thinking and it goes right to voicemail. I immediately start crying, or maybe just continue crying, I don't know which. "It's me. Please pick up if you're there. I know you must be angry. I've been a shitty daughter, but please, please come to Bloomington, Illinois, if and when you get this. We're at the hospital. In the ER. Something terrible has happened to Lucas. I know I screwed up, but I need you, Daddy. Please."

Why didn't he answer? If he's this angry, I fear where he'll send me next. Colorado, like Monika? A maximum-security residential treatment center in the Yukon?

The next call I make is to Declan. His strong, steady voice calms me after some initial hysterics.

"It's going to be okay. Tell me what to do," he says.

"We need to get a hold of Lucas's parents. Tell them to call the ER at the hospital in Bloomington, Illinois. Lucas stopped breathing. He went into cardiac arrest."

What if he dies? I'm the opposite of a good luck charm. I'm the person who forgets to pack the parachute on a tandem skydive. In a constant state of freefall and taking everyone down with me.

"Oh, fuck. I was afraid of something like this. The docs told him he shouldn't be wrestling. At any weight and maybe not ever. He's—"

"He has bulimia. You can say it. His resting heart was super low, like in the fifties, and he was dehydrated. His parents need to get here," I say.

Not everyone suffering from malnutrition looks skeletal. But after what Dec just said, I'm worried he's done some irreparable damage. The heart is a muscle, I can hear Maeve say.

"On it. Stay strong. I'll call you back," Declan says.

I disconnect and approach the nurse's station.

"Excuse me. Can you tell me what's happening with my friend, Lucas Polizzi? His parents should be calling soon. Can I see him? I don't want him to be alone."

I'm ushered through the ER, greeted by the scents of Lysol and pee, the bleats of hospital machines. Immediately, I'm whisked back to Children's and River House. The shuffling cards, the meal trays stacked on carts, the wasted hours spent in my bed. I think of Maeve watching her game shows and wonder if she misses me, and Monika. I hope to see her again someday when we're both in a better place.

Some patients are behind curtains; others, like Lucas, are in a small room with a floor-to-ceiling glass wall on one side. My knees buckle and I have to grab the door frame when I see him, eyes closed, attached to a heart monitor and IV, lost in the oversized hospital gown that makes him look like a little boy in his father's pajamas.

There's a nurse standing at his bedside with a laptop on a rolling cart. "Gemma?"

I nod.

"Come on in. He's been asking for you."

I release the oxygen weighing like lead in my lungs.

"He's awake?"

"Of course I'm awake. How else could I have been asking for you?" Lucas says.

I walk beside the bed and take his hand. His eyes open and he tries to smile.

"Lucas, I'm so sorry—"

He pulls his hand from mine and puts a finger to my lips,

then closes his eyes again. "No talking. We're fine. Not normal. Not even close. But fine."

The nurse pulls over the only chair in the room and positions it behind me.

"Sit, hon. It's going to be a while," she says.

"I'm not going anywhere," I say.

She points me toward the restroom and hands me the TV remote, then drapes a blanket over my shoulders and leaves in one swift motion, before I can thank her.

I position the chair as close to the bed as possible and lean my forehead against the mattress edge, hyperaware of my new role as the person who keeps a bedside vigil. I think of how my dad must have felt, and Monika's parents, and the fake promise that put us all in this predicament. That Skinny will make us happy, and the long list of ways to get us there.

What I Ate Today and eating disorder recovery videos that are basically how-tos. Cutting weight, shredding, and other athletic terms for saying "starve yourself." Ads for Keto, Weight Watchers, low-calorie, low-carb, Slim Fast, Jenny Craig, Nutrisystem, South Beach, Lean Cuisine, Noom, Paleo, Intermittent Fasting, Mediterranean, Plant-Based, Atkins, Zone. And don't get me started on the fashion industry. Heroin chic? What the actual fuck? Promoting multiple ways to kill yourself for the sake of a photo shoot. Or how about that motherfucker Balanchine and his ideas about what the correct body weight for a ballet dancer should be? Who are these men who think they know what's best for a woman's body?

Skinny is a fraud, I think. No wonder it doesn't exist on a map. It's not real and chasing it will leave you hollow not happy, or healthy. Problem is, once people like me and Lucas buy into it, the spiral can be long and deadly before we find a path out.

I turn on the overhead TV and search the channels, determined to find the Food Network just to spite my fucking therapist. Ex-fucking therapist. I'd would have loved to have seen her face when she found out I'd escaped. This one's for you, I think when I land on *Diners, Drive-In and Dives,* and proceed to binge on food porn. The last thing I remember is Guy Fieri biting into a fish taco before falling into a twilight sleep—the only kind I have in hospitals—and dream of Dad.

"Why, Gemma, why can't you eat? One bite. That's all I'm asking. We'll take it one bite at a time."

We're at the kitchen table. My untouched plate is in front of me. I don't look at the food. I don't look at him. I don't look at anything. All I can see is blurry white skin cells passing in front of my pupils.

"Gemma?"

I can't talk.

"Gemma?"

I can't. I can't. I can't.

"Gemma!"

I stand up. Run to my room. Slam the door and lock it, then let out a scream that begins deep inside my hollow gut and rises until it makes my head and teeth hurt. I cover my ears to block out his pounding on the door. "No! No! No!" I scream it over and over again until the lock pops with either a paper clip or the wire made to do just that that hangs on a key chain with the backdoor key, and I crumble to the floor.

Gemma.

I hear my name in a whisper and it wakes me. It's not Dad. Why would it be? Why would he ever want me to come home again? He shouldn't have to live like that. No one should.

It takes my brain a few more seconds to emerge from the memory of my last night at home before an ambulance transported me from my school to a local hospital and Dad took me to Children's.

Lucas' voice finally pushes through the haze. Murmuring from a one-sided conversation.

Dec, I'm fine, really. She's fine too. Sleeping. If anything happens...she might need a friend. Dec, I'm serious. If you hurt her, even if I'm dead, I'll kill you.

"If you die, I'll kill *you*," I say.

"I thought you were sleeping."

I put out my hand. "Phone."

Lucas hands it over. "Dramatic much?" I say to him. "Hey, Declan. Sorry to interrupt this session of the care and maintenance of Gemma Leonardo. Can we call you back?"

I disconnect without waiting for an answer.

"What was that?" I ask.

Lucas lifts one shoulder. Not even a full shrug.

"Worry about your own heart," I say. "Why didn't you tell me the doctors at Children's said you shouldn't be wrestling as a lightweight? Maybe not at all."

"Then I would have had to admit it was true."

"And give me some credit. Declan? Seriously? If I fall for anyone, it's going to be you. Idiot."

"That was both harsh and encouraging."

"I'm sorry for being harsh," I say.

I lean down and kiss his lips.

"Can I ask you something?"

"Hm?"

"Did you give me mouth to mouth when I stopped breathing? Because I got a flashback just now."

I laugh and shake my head. "Try to get some rest. Your heart rate jumped up to ninety." I wave the burner phone at him. "I'm going to try my dad again."

Lucas grabs my hand. "Gemma?"

I love you. He doesn't need to say it.

"I know. Me too," I say out loud.

"Ride or die, right? Only now, after most careful consideration, I'd prefer not to die."

"Me too," I say.

When I return from the lounge down the hall, there's two women leaning over his bed, one with long dark hair, the same color as mine, and a familiar silhouette. In that moment I'm unsure if I'm seeing the past or some future version of myself. I blink, thinking I'm seeing double in the low light, and bring my eyes into focus. There are still two women there. But then one turns toward the door, toward me, and a warmth, like stepping from the shadows into the bright sunlight, falls over me. My body hums. "Mom?"

She tilts her head. "Lucas's mom, honey," she says gently.

I shake away my confusion. "Right, Lucas's mom. That's what I meant."

But my mistake renders me speechless and immobile as she rushes toward me and, undaunted by my awkwardness, pulls me into her arms.

"I'm so sorry," I say it over and over again, thinking she must hate me, the girl who almost killed her only child. But she pulls me tighter, enveloping me with a mother's love, my mother's love. Because despite knowing that she couldn't possibly be here, it's her breath I feel, her voice I hear when she repeats over and over, "It's all right, sweetie. Everything is going to be all right. I'm here."

"Hello, Mom! Your son's over here in a hospital bed."

"Shush!" she snaps at him over my shoulder.

When we finally separate, I can see now how much she resembles Lucas. Same high cheekbones and olive skin, same round eyes. "Look at you," she says, taking my face in her hands. "You're beautiful. No wonder my son ran away with you. I would have too."

It's a generous thing to say to someone so undeserving of kindness. She must still be in shock. I try again to apologize, but she won't have it and looks like she's about to say something more when we're interrupted by the attending physician who explains what tests need to be performed.

"After the CT scan, we're going to transfer him to pediatric cardiology as soon as there's a bed available," the doctor says.

"Back where I started. And must they say pediatric?" Lucas says.

"Listen, mister," his mom says.

I take it as my cue to give them some privacy. Phone in hand, I back up toward the door. "I'm going to try my dad again. I keep calling but he won't pick up."

"That's because he's already here," his voice says from behind me.

I'm crying before I can even turn around. Dad stands in the doorway, strong hands clenched at his sides. He's a burly guy with a slight paunch and longish beard that has unintentionally become cool. He opens his arms and I rush toward him, hugging him with a ferocity that surprises us both. "Do you know how much I've missed these hugs?" he says.

I do. Because I've missed them more.

"Don't you ever do something like this again. Do you hear me? There may be only two of us, but we're a family and we need to stick together, you and me. Got it?"

His voice cracks and I nearly break in half.

I nod into his chest, inhale his aftershave and the heavy-duty detergent he uses for all his shop clothes to get the grease stains out. "I thought you were mad at me."

"I'm furious. But not at you. At what happened to you." He stops to keep from crying. "And okay, maybe I'm a little mad that you didn't call me first. But mad or not, I love you, baby girl. I left for the airport the second your grandmother called and told me where you were. A snow delay, two flights, and a taxi, but I got here as soon as I could."

"Same." Lucas's mom dabs her eyes. "We moved heaven and earth to get to you two."

"We are so f-ing grounded," Lucas says.

"Got that right," his mom says.

An orderly arrives to take Lucas and his mom to radiology for his CT scan.

Lucas turns to me. "So," he says, "before you go—"

"I'm not going anywhere. I'll be here when you come back from your scan and every day after that, even when I'm back in New Jersey."

"In Nutley?"

"No jokes."

"No jokes."

Dad claps his hands together. "How about we find the cafeteria?" Dad asks.

My body tenses and there's a slight buzz in the back of my skull as my synapses threaten overload. I can't.

But then I see the look on his face—the fear, the anticipation—and for the first time in a long time, I'm willing to try. Today, tomorrow, the next day. I'm going to try, and keep trying, because trying won't kill me, but not trying will. Now that I know what it's like to be the one beside the hospital bed, holding the hand of someone you love, while something rages inside their body that you don't fully understand and can't fix or control, but it's threatening to steal them from you. I won't put Dad through that again.

"Yes, I'm starving," I say, and the relief I see on his face makes it all worth it.

New Year's Eve, Eve

Holly and Marmee race from my bedroom toward the staircase the minute they hear the car door slam. I know it's Lucas. I've been keeping an eye on his dot, growing ever closer, on the phone app that connects us. I like being alerted to his movements. Lucas left the hospital. Lucas left home. Lucas left school. We don't seem so far apart on a phone screen.

It's the same with Chester. He's made his way from the vet's office to a wildlife rescue in DeKalb County, Illinois, where he gets more than his fair share of screen time on their Critter Cam. No doubt because of his undeniable adorableness! He's gotten bigger and wilder and found his people among three other orphaned raccoons and a Sheepadoodle named Sid. My own dogs will never replace Chester, but it helps knowing he has a home.

From my bedroom window, I get an aerial view of the Impala 2.0—complete with a shiny blue paint job and gleaming bumpers—that sits at the curb. Lucas and Declan make their way up the short walk.

Marmee, named for the mom in *Little Women*, turns circles as she waits by the gated staircase. She stops and nudges my knee softly when I arrive. I pat her between her floppy ears and kiss her nose as I bend down to scoop up Holly, her three-legged pup, who's still learning to navigate going up and down stairs.

"You're a good momma," I say.

As soon as we hit the landing, Holly wriggles to be put down and I smile as mother and daughter skid to a stop at the front door, tails wagging, noses snuffling. They smell friendlies.

"Clear the way, girls," I say.

I only get the door open a crack before the dogs rush into Lucas's arms.

"Santa must have been here," Lucas says.

I cock my head. "Save it. I know you read my letter. That's a federal offense you know."

Lucas texted my father and told him I'd asked Santa for a dog for Christmas. Dad surprised me a few days before Christmas Eve with a trip to the shelter. The second I saw her, I knew. She didn't need four legs. She needed to be loved exactly the way she was.

Holly was meant for me and so was Marmee, though she was more of a bonus. She was a breeder dog who'd never known life outside of a cage. Imagine never rolling around in the grass, sniffing trees and flowers, or chasing chipmunks and squirrels. Mom and baby were abandoned because some a-hole considered them worthless. It didn't take much to convince Dad we needed to adopt them both.

"Can I help it if I have X-ray vision?" Lucas says.

He kisses me sweetly on the lips, then dives to the floor to roughhouse with the dogs while Declan gives me a side hug.

"You didn't know you were dating a superhero, huh?" Declan says.

"We're not dating," Lucas and I say at the same time.

"I can see that. Like I said, old married couple," Declan says.

We're really not dating, or talking, or whatever the labels are. There's no name for what we are, not yet. Right now we're the person most invested in making sure the other gets better. Each other's safe light. The clarifying lens through which we can see our true selves when the wires in our hearts and brains go haywire, and they will.

Recovery is a process, but one we will never have to go through alone. I love Lucas for who he is but also for showing me who I am, a beautiful human being deserving of love.

"X-ray vision and a bionic heart." Lucas pats his chest, which Holly takes as an invitation to pounce and plop the squeaky toy he brought her on his face.

He doesn't have a bionic heart. But he does have a built-in defibrillator. Should his heart ever stop again—God forbid—that gadget will give it the jumpstart it needs. Starving, cutting weight, purging, it all takes its toll on the body. But with time, some of that damage can be reversed.

"Congrats on Columbia," Declan says. "Lucas told me."

"Thanks! Dad and I are talking about me deferring for a year so I can continue with intensive out-patient," I admit without shame. "Going to finish out senior year with homeschooling."

I lift Holly off Lucas's chest and kiss her nose, happy there are no follow-up questions. That's the beautiful thing about having friends who know all your secrets. No need for awkward explanations.

My new therapist and I talked about how the pursuit of perfection causes us to hide the parts of ourselves we're afraid to let people see and that can lead to isolation and loneliness. That's why she suggested I audit an in-person class at a local college in addition to homeschooling. "You need to be around people your age. Give yourself a chance to figure out your likes and dislikes, without being graded or judged," Tessa told me.

That's her name, Tessa. I had tried four other therapists, before connecting with her literally thirty seconds into our first meeting.

I called her Dr. Rivas when I stepped into her office and she said, "What, am I a dentist? Call me Tessa."

Done.

She also told me she only has one rule. "We don't talk about food. I want to talk about you."

Fuck, yeah. Finally!

"Where do I sign?" I joked.

Anyway, Tessa is one of several people on "Team Gemma," as Dad likes to call it. He's threatening to get T-shirts made and I'm, like, "No." I'm also seeing an adolescent medical doctor and nutritionist, plus I'm taking up drums. It was either that or ax throwing. I think Mom would approve of my choice. The team agrees I need an outlet to quiet my brain and I'm relatively certain Dad wouldn't be on board with me drinking whiskey.

Plus, who needs Jack Daniels when you have Marmee and Holly. They've made me braver—more open to making connections with other dog owners, or in some cases, rekindling old ones. Two days after Christmas, while walking Marmee, I ran into Gus Manetti, the kid who saved me from lunch table-loneliness and my longtime crush. Home from Rutgers for the holidays and long break, I assumed.

"Gemma?" He was in the driveway lifting groceries from the trunk of his mom's car. He had five bags spooled over one arm.

Marmee took tentative steps toward him, tail wagging. He put out his free hand to let her sniff. My canine icebreaker.

"Hey, Gus. Meet Marmee," I said. Tongue-tied no more.

"I wasn't sure if that was you coming down the block," he said.

Haymitch tried to ruin my reunion. *Because you're getting fatter. Unrecognizable.*

Gus explained before I spiraled. "I didn't know you guys had a dog. You looked out of context, you know?"

It'd been a long time since we'd seen each other in any context, but I explained how we just rescued her and her three-legged pup, Holly, and said he should stop by and meet her. Gus said he would, then told me his mom had been worried about me. She hadn't seen me at the bus stop in months.

"I was in the hospital but I'm better now."

"No shit? Really? You're okay now? I mean you look great—" I nodded. "Really."

His genuine concern brought tears to my eyes. I nodded toward the five bags of groceries still dangling from one hand. "I should let you bring those in before your mom comes looking."

"Gemma! Is that you?"

Gus smiled. "Too late."

Mrs. Manetti called from the open screen door. "Merry Christmas, hon! We've been so worried about you!"

"Ma, I told her. I'll be right there."

Then Gus gave me a hug with his grocery-free arm.

"When can we stop by to meet the puppy?"

"Anytime," I said.

Marmee was pulling and I started walking. "We never stopped looking out for you, Gemma. You know that, right?"

I nodded. I didn't. But I do now.

Marmee barks at the door as Dad's truck pulls into the driveway. Right on time. He said he'd be home early to watch the dogs since I've leaving for Dillsburg with Lucas and Dec. The pickle drop is tomorrow. I didn't want to leave him alone on New Year's Eve, but he insisted. I think he's dating someone but not quite ready to tell me, which is fine. Secretly I'm thrilled that Santa came through with my second wish, for Dad to find someone to love and not have to worry about me anymore. I understand now that those things are not mutually exclusive, that a healthy dose of worry for the people we love may wind up being the thing that saves their life. More than once.

Declan spies Dad circling the Impala, giving it a onceover.

"I'm gonna talk shop with your dad," he says. "Meet you out there when you're ready."

"I got you something," Lucas says as soon as Declan goes outside.

"You already sent me a Christmas present. Stop wasting money on me," I say.

"Where's your phone?"

I pull it from my back pocket. It's been wiped clean of all social media apps, but I'm happy to have information at my fingertips again. Everything in moderation. Hamlet got it wrong. Obviously, since, spoiler alert, he dies. Things can be good or bad. Thinking helps you figure that shit out.

My text pings.

"Make sure the volume is turned up," he says.

Lucas sent me a video. It's grainy but the sound is unmistakable. *Thump, thump. Thump, thump. Thump, thump.* I know a beating heart when I hear one.

"I love it. I'll keep it forever."

"I know you will. That's why I gave it to you."

Outside, Declan hands me the keys like he did back in October at the junk yard.

I shake my head. "I'm not going to drive your car, especially now that it's all fixed up and looking beautiful."

Dad smiles. "You like it?"

"I love it."

I do. Not only because it looks so much better, but because it is the place Lucas and I spent so much time together. Sometimes home is a car.

"I'm happy to hear you say that," Dad says. "Because it's yours."

"Dad, are you serious? You bought me a car? You really should not reward my recent bad behavior."

"You'll need something to get back and forth to your poetry class and I don't get many opportunities to take a used car on a 900-mile test drive."

After retrieving the Impala from the garage where it had been towed, and being reunited with my precious atlas, Dad and I made the long journey home from Illinois to New Jersey. Fifteen hours straight through, with pit stops. Plenty of time for some long overdue father/daughter talks.

Some conversations will only ever happen inside a car. It's like this sacred, moving space existing both nowhere and everywhere all at once that promises at every turn to keep your secrets safe inside.

"Thanks, Dad. Happy New Year!"

"Happy New Year, kiddo. Drive safe and come back this time, all right?"

He laughs and I kiss him on the cheek. "Deal."

I take the keys from Declan and slide into the front seat, where Lucas is already cuing up the eight-track. "Kool and the Gang?" he asks.

"No dancing," I say.

Declan yawns and stretches in the back seat. "I'm going to nap back here if you two don't mind."

Lucas turns to me as he pops in the jumbo cassette. "Know where you're going?"

"Not exactly," I say.

It's true. And that's okay. Because this time, I don't have to figure it out alone.

Gemma Leonardo
Intro. To Poetry
Prof. Bernard Asbell

Skinny is Not a Place

Skinny is a fraud.
A four-letter word stretching to six
Take away one "n," the why
And it's just skin, taut across bone.

Like fairy floss round paper cones,
A confectioner's artifice on hollow spoons.
Skinny could never masquerade as strength,
Or imitate the warm, supple weight of love.

Skinny is just a word. Like fat, or fingernails,
Hair or eyes. Brown or green. Arm or leg.
It cannot define a person,
Pretend to know their heart.

AUTHOR'S NOTE

While writing this note I realized how much books and the human body have in common. This book is very personal for me. I've spent years working on it and have put my heart into every page. But once this novel goes out into the world, it will be vulnerable. It's the risk every author—every artist—takes when they pour themselves into their work, hoping their creations will bring about connection and positive change. Maybe that's why we call it a body of work? Unsolicited comments, opinions, and criticism about art are expected, welcomed even. But speaking freely about someone's physical appearance—positive or negative—is not. When I was nine years old my pediatrician told me that if I did not lose weight he would be forced to write "obese" on my chart. He put me on my first diet and told me I'd "look better" if I weighed less. It was my first lesson in the hurtful way words could be used to describe the human body. The word "obese" didn't shame me, the way he said it did. When he told me I would "look better" if I were smaller, what I heard was people would like me better. And so began my very complicated relationship with food. Eating disorders and disordered eating have had a profound and devastating effect on my life. When I was writing this book, some of the early feedback I received was "No one wants to read about eating disorders." This is not a book about eating disorders. It's a book about two teens, Gemma and Lucas, on a journey to find love and acceptance. Yes, they both have a potentially deadly disease—eating disorders have the second highest mortality rate of any mental illness. But their diseases do not define them. Nor does the shape and size of their bodies. An estimated 30 million Americans will experience an eating disorder at some point in the lives. Eating disorders affect people of every age, race, gender, sex, body type, and sexual orientation. Anorexia, bulimia, orthorexia, ARFID, and all forms of disordered eating are misunderstood diseases, but it is my hope that someday we will be as comfortable talking about them as we are about cancer, diabetes, heart disease, addiction, and all other mental illnesses. People struggling to recover from disordered eating deserve love, support, respect, and understanding, not shame, judgement, or blame.

For help and information about eating disorders.

Project HEAL theprojectheal.org

Equip Health 855-387-4378 www.equip.health

National Eating Disorders Association nationaleatingdisorders. org

Call 911 or go directly to a hospital emergency room if you're experiencing a life-threatening emergency.

Call or text 988 for the Suicide & Crisis Lifeline if you are in crisis. Available 24/7. Chat at 988lifeline.org

ACKNOWLEDGMENTS

I would like to thank the following people for their time, talents, and support. No one writes a book alone and I appreciate everyone that helped me on this journey. Melissa Azarian, Lauren Bjorkman and her husband Dr. Pelle Bjorkman, Adriana Calderon, Maris Degener, Val Emmich, Nicole Fegan, Jen Mann, Jackie Medina, Becky Osowski, Annette Pollert Morgan, Kim Murray, Mary Pan and her husband Dr. Wilbur Pan, Lisa Reiss, Jaynie Royal and C. B. Royal and the amazing team at Fitzroy Books/Regal House Publishing, Holly Schindler, and Kerry Sparks. Love and thanks to Mike and Carley and my entire family for allowing me to dream.